S0-EGR-202

Dear Reader:

Everyone here at JOVE and all our authors are simply thrilled by the enthusiastic reception you've given to SECOND CHANCE AT LOVE!

We have lots of marvelous love stories coming up for the fall and winter by both seasoned pros and the brand-new talent we're very proud to be able to present. Our goal is to give you wholesome, heart-warming, yet exciting romances that are a pleasure to read. So, of course, your opinion about how well we're doing is very important to us, and we love to have your reactions to our SECOND CHANCE AT LOVE novels. Do let us hear from *you*!

Again, thanks for so warmly welcoming SECOND CHANCE AT LOVE. Your response has encouraged and inspired us.

With every good wish,

Carolyn Nichols

Carolyn Nichols
SECOND CHANCE AT LOVE
Jove Publications, Inc.
200 Madison Avenue
New York, New York 10016

"You're trying to seduce me, aren't you?" Nick said...

"You're trying to keep me from working on the book you're so afraid of—the book that would reveal the truth about your marriage..."

Christine ran to her bedroom. Too late she realized he had followed her. As she turned to confront him, he gave one brutal lunge and pushed her, sprawling, back across her bed.

"You're playing with fire, little girl," he said savagely, throwing himself on one knee beside her. "You've known how hard it's been for me to keep my hands off you. I've wanted you from that first moment I saw you. Now you're trying a dangerous game, one you know nothing about. And you're liable to get hurt."

He looked down into her pleading eyes with no sympathy, then slowly, menacingly, his mouth pressed ruthlessly upon hers...

Second Chance at Love™

ALOHA, YESTERDAY

MEREDITH KINGSTON

A JOVE BOOK

Copyright © 1981 by Meredith Kingston

All rights reserved. No part of this publication may be reproduced or transmitted in any form or by any means, electronic or mechanical, including photocopy, recording, or any information storage and retrieval system, without permission in writing from the publisher.

Requests for permission to make copies of any part of the work should be mailed to: Permissions, "Second Chance at Love," Jove Publications, Inc., 200 Madison Avenue, New York, NY 10016

First Jove edition published September 1981

First printing

"Second Chance at Love" and the butterfly emblem are trademarks belonging to Jove Publications, Inc.

Printed in the United States of America

Jove books are published by Jove Publications, Inc.,
200 Madison Avenue, New York, NY 10016

CHAPTER ONE

CHRISTINE PARKED HER mink-colored Mercedes coupe precisely between the marked lines on the pavement, then checked her appointment book, put it back into her purse, and got out. She was familiar with this parking lot because it was near the Waikiki Shell, and when she brought her mother-in-law to the summer concerts of the Honolulu Symphony, they parked in this same spot every Saturday night and then walked through Kapiolani Park to their seats.

This time, however, she headed across the traffic of Kapahulu Avenue toward the entrance of the Queen Kapiolani Hotel. The thought of the last concert she'd attended brought a scrap of music to her mind, and before she could restrain herself, she was whistling the tune and tapping her hand on the broad leather surface of her shoulder bag in time to it. Then she remembered how often David's mother had to remind her that it is unladylike to whistle, and she slowly plodded up the front steps of the hotel, the melody dead on her lips.

"Excuse me, ma'am." A delivery boy bumped her with a long box he was carrying as he hurried past her into the lobby.

Of course he called her ma'am. No one ever called her miss. With her stiff black cotton dress and her light brown hair tightly twisted into a knot at the back of her neck, she

1

was easily mistaken for a woman far beyond her twenty-five years of age.

She welcomed the dark atmosphere of the old-fashioned lobby, decorated with ornate green wallpaper and chandeliers that looked like the old kerosene lamps of the whalers who once frequented Hawaii. Although the hotel was fairly new, it tried to recapture the mood of the islands a century ago, during the Monarchy period when King Kalakaua, the last reigning king of these islands, had dedicated the huge park across the street to his beloved consort, Queen Kapiolani. Christine stood before the stately life-sized portrait of the Queen for a moment as she rummaged through her purse in search of the scrap of paper on which she had jotted down the room number she needed.

This hotel was one of her favorites, but it seemed odd to her that a world-famous author had chosen such a little-known place to stay. She could picture Nicolas Carruthers enjoying the super-luxury of the Kahala Hilton, where the Queen of England and the Emperor of Japan had been well pleased, or the traditional old Halekulani on Waikiki Beach, or the glamorous towers of the Ilikai. But this hotel was more the style of someone very familiar with Honolulu.

At last she resigned herself to the fact that she couldn't find the note even in her systematically arranged handbag and went to the registration desk. The clerk gave her the room number, then added that the man she was looking for was in his "usual penthouse suite." So, she now knew that he enjoyed the high-priced pleasures of life in a suite, and that he was a frequent enough visitor to the Hawaiian Islands that he had discovered this hotel for himself and had one special room that was a favorite.

The door to his room, like all the others, had an imposing full-color reproduction of the seal of the state of Hawaii over it, and Christine felt intimidated as she stood at the door, considering the international reputation of the writer she was about to meet. She wondered what he would be like. Since he had already written several books, he was certainly not a young man. He was probably rather world-weary and sophisticated. But she hoped he would be fatherly and kind to her, so that their sessions together would be as tolerable as possible.

She couldn't imagine what it was going to be like, being interviewed by an experienced journalist. She only knew that she had much she wanted to tell him about David's bravery and courage, his dreams for a better world, his dedication to his military career. David's life could serve as a model for younger men, inspiring them and showing them the way to a life of action and commitment. For this reason she had agreed to help out with this project. She didn't look forward to the hours of discussing personal details of her husband's life and her own with a total stranger, but the family had convinced her she owed it to David and to the Navy men who would profit by it.

As she reached up to knock she glanced at her watch and realized that she was a few minutes early, as usual. She kept her life so fastidiously programmed that she often found herself ahead of schedule. But she rapped at the door anyway, still picturing in her mind the kindly old author who would help her through the ordeal ahead.

After her second loud knock on the door it flew open, and immediately she felt her entire face turn scarlet with a blush of shock, for in the moment before she averted her eyes to a study of the carpet at her feet, she had gained in one startled glance the impression that a young man was standing before her without a stitch of clothing on.

"Oh, come now, young lady. Certainly you don't live in Honolulu without seeing an occasional bare chest."

Christine lifted her head toward the sound of the imperious heavy voice, keeping her eyes tightly closed until she heard him say with a booming laugh, "I have a towel on, your sense of modesty is safe."

She opened her eyes and took in the overpowering vision of a man who could have been a tanned Hawaiian Prince emerging from the warm Polynesian seas.

"I'm sorry," she stammered. "I'm looking for Nicolas Carruthers. I think I've come too early."

"That you have, but come on in. I don't run my life by the clock. You're here, so let's get this meeting started."

With that he turned around and walked into the room, obviously expecting her to follow him inside. She glanced about the empty hallway to make sure no one had seen this unexpected greeting, and then decided her only choice was to step inside and close the door quickly behind her.

The man hitched the towel a bit tighter around himself and said, "Since our meeting wasn't until two o'clock, I thought I'd have time for a quick shower. I never dreamed that the poor little Widow Hanover was so in need of excitement that she would barge in here ahead of time and try to sneak a peek at me."

"Mr. Carruthers—I assume you are Mr. Carruthers—I have already apologized for being early. Now . . ."

"Stop blustering, my dear. You've blown your cover. All your beautifully applied self-control has fallen in a heap around your ankles."

Christine knew he was right. She was fumbling with her purse, her eyes darting around the room in a frantic attempt to avoid looking at the man standing before her, taunting her. She took a deep breath.

"I am Christine Hanover, and I am here at the instruction of my brother-in-law Andrew Hanover. I gather he and his daughter have not yet arrived."

"I am not in the habit of showering in a threesome. No, they are not here yet."

Nicolas Carruthers had planted himself squarely in the middle of the room and seemed to be as comfortably in control of the situation as if he had been attired in full evening dress. Now that she had regained some of her composure, Christine took a frank and admiring look at him. He was one of the most dramatically handsome men she'd ever met, and obviously was just as convinced of that fact as she was. She judged him to be about thirty-five. He had a beige hotel towel precariously tucked around his waist, and with both clenched fists resting on his hips seemed to be offering his body to her for inspection.

As her eyes moved upward across his broad chest, where

his deep tan was shadowed with a sprinkling of curling dark hair, he stepped closer to her, so that by the time her eyes had come to rest comfortably on his face, he was near enough to reach out and touch.

If she had expected the appraising and searching eyes of the author, he satisfied those journalistic prerequisites, but his probing look came from eyes so unexpectedly blue that she could not break their lock on her. His dark hair was still drenched and dripping in rivulets down his neck, but he seemed unconcerned as he stood watching her with a curious expression.

"I can't believe what I'm seeing," he said with a trace of a laugh in his voice. "The Widow Hanover, all dressed in black, buttoned up as primly as the early missionaries in their Mother Hubbards."

"At least, Mr. Carruthers, I am dressed."

"You don't approve of my costume?"

"No more than you approve of mine."

She turned away from him and walked toward the sliding glass window that opened up one side of the room to an awesome view of the park below.

"Perhaps the solution is for both of us to be dressed exactly the same. Then we can meet as equals, without the interference of misleading wardrobes. If we could only free you of that imposing image you try to assume." As he was speaking she could hear him moving around the room, and then she heard him walk right up behind her.

With horror she felt him reach out and touch her at the waist, and she jumped with surprise—she was so unused to such familiarity. She started to turn around and reprimand him when she felt his hands reach around in front of her to place the towel, sarong-like, around her hips over her dress.

"Now, isn't that more appropriate for a beautiful young island girl?" he said so seductively that she unwittingly caught his mood.

She looked down at herself, observing his hands so tightly clasped around her waist that her body now transformed the loose black dress into a curving hourglass shape.

She had wide hips and a generous bust, but they only showed to advantage when her tiny waist set them off by contrast, and she rarely dressed in such a way.

The immodest little patch of towel seemed amusing against the severe black chasteness of her dress, and she began to smile at the incongruity. Then suddenly a ripple of shock froze the new smile in place as she realized that his huge tan hands were holding in place around her the towel he had been wearing. Which meant that he was now standing behind her wearing nothing at all!

She tried to push the towel in bunches into his fingers, keeping her back toward him, but as she did so he slowly released his hold on it so that she was left with it in her own hands. And then she heard him walk away from her, chuckling as he stolled casually around his suite.

"Now that's more like it. I just thought you might be hiding a beautiful figure under that dreary dress of yours. Of course, the effect would be a little more provocative if there was only bronze skin beneath your swaying grass skirt."

"Why, how dare you!" she sputtered.

"How about a little hula dance, honey?" he laughed.

"Do you know who you're talking to?" she demanded in a hoarse whisper of rage. She had never been treated in such a demeaning way. "If this is your idea of a joke . . ." she began. But it was not easy talking to this infuriating stranger while keeping herself so resolutely turned away from him.

"I think it is a wonderful joke. Why don't you turn around here and see?"

"I will not turn around. What's more, I'm not going to stay here a moment longer." She began inching her way around the room, always facing the wall, feeling foolish as she tried to get to the door without encountering the naked body of the writer who was probably strutting around behind her back.

As she neared the entry area of the suite, she heard Nicolas Carruther's voice on her left and she knew that he was standing right at the door, blocking her exit, saying with that honey-coated teasing voice she had come to despise, "Aw, don't you like my little trick? I just wanted to see if you were human, that's all. I wanted to see if there was any way to warm up that ice water that flows through your veins." He must have leaned close to her then, for his voice came from so close to her ear that she gave a start. "See, I got you down off of that high horse real fast."

"You are contemptible," she blurted out, hoping that by unleashing some of her anger she could calm herself enough to plan her next move. But she found that she was hurling her accusations meant for the author squarely at a framed portrait of Captain Cook, the discoverer of Hawaii, which graced a side wall in the entryway to the right of the door. "Your attitude is degrading, and lacking in proper respect, and I've never been . . ."

"What a way to talk to Captain Cook!"

Christine had to admit that her performance was ludicrous, telling off a painting, and she stopped her tirade to smile in exasperation. After all, she assured herself, she was a grown woman, had been married, and had no reason to be so embarrassed by this situation. Once she had caught her breath she would simply turn around and face the naked man, take him by surprise and demand he let her out of this damnable trap he'd set for her for his own amusement. Then, when she had him off guard, she would bolt for the door.

With an adventurous toss of her head that brought several strands of her light hair loose from the chignon, she turned around to face him, and then both of them began to laugh, Christine releasing all the tension of the last few moments in deep, satisfying gulps of laughter, heartier than any she'd enjoyed in a long time. For now she saw that Nicolas Carruthers was still firmly bound in the towel she'd first encountered him in; he'd simply grabbed up an extra one from nearby with which to tease her.

"I thought . . . I thought . . ." she tried to say.

"I know what you thought. And I knew you'd have a fit. Why, watching you inch your way around the walls was worth the price of admission."

"And then I stood there telling off Captain Cook," she choked, stopping to catch her breath in between the uncontrollable bursts of laughter. She grabbed the towel she was holding by one corner and remembering a trick she learned back in grade school, she flipped out with a painful snap that caught Nicolas Carruthers on the knee just below the edge of his covering towel. She said playfully, "Take that, you practical joker."

"Ouch," he yelped. "I'll get you for that," and he started toward her with such a lunge that the towel around his waist came untied, and he made a grab for it just before it fell off of him. They both erupted into a new fit of laughter as they leaned helplessly against the walls of the small anteroom for support.

Just then there was a loud rapping sound, and Christine knew that whoever was outside could hear their laughter even through the heavy wood of the door.

"Now I guess we'll find out if your brother-in-law appreciates the joke," Carruthers said, reaching for the door handle.

"Oh, no. Wait a minute!" Christine said sharply, coming back to her senses. What would Andrew think, seeing her this way, laughing in a way he'd never heard her laugh, cavorting around a hotel room with a half-clad giant of a man? He would never see any humor in such a situation.

But Carruthers had already opened the door, and with relief Christine saw it was a white-coated houseboy. He carried a beautifully carved tray made from monkeypod, the tropical tree that supplies much of the wood for ornamental items in the Pacific. The exquisite tray was heaped with fresh fruit.

"Compliments of management, sir. She say we hope you enjoy another fine stay with us. *E kipi mai*."

The writer patted at the nonexistent pockets on his towel-sarong. "Catch you later, Aka, okay?"

The boy put the platter down on a small game table near the window and left with a smile at the two of them, apparently satisfied he'd get his tip at a more convenient time.

"I wonder what he thought," Christine mused, now more

comfortable in the presence of the man she had not trusted just a few moments ago.

"I imagine hotel employees see enough goings-on not to be very shocked at seeing a very properly attired gentleman having a polite discussion with an uptight widow lady."

Christine was not offended by his description of her. She was very conscious of the impression she gave people.

"I'm afraid my brother-in-law would have been scandalized."

"Since I can see that it is important to you that your immaculate reputation be preserved, I will be glad to go put on some clothes before he gets here with his impressionable young daughter."

"I think it would get our meeting off to a much better start," she said with a grateful smile. "And it would save a lot of explanations. You see, since David's death his family has been very protective of me. They watch over me, and worry about me."

"Just what are they so worried about? That you might have a good time?"

"You know what I mean. This is a Navy town, despite its being a pleasure haven for tourists. And Navy people are all very close. The Hanovers just want to make sure no one gets any wrong ideas about the way I live. They have some very strict rules of propriety."

"And since you are, by marriage, a Hanover, you have to live by those rules, is that it?"

"It's not such a bad way to live," she said defensively.

Nicolas Carruthers looked at her expensive leather purse and matching shoes, the gold watch at her wrist, and the diamond studs that decorated her pierced ears. "I'm sure it is quite a luxurious way to live," he said, and then with a twisted grin in her direction to let her know what he thought of the bargain she'd struck with her life, he left the room to go and dress.

Christine paced the large, airy living room of the suite restlessly after the dynamic presence of the writer had left it, somehow, desolate. Like the rest of the hotel, this room was furnished in the style of the Kalakaua Dynasty, with groupings of bentwood wicker chairs that were replicas of Old Hawaii furniture.

She sat down in one of the chairs at the table, one with a tall fan-shaped back next to the window, and admired the platter of fruit. There were rose-colored guavas, wild bananas, avocados from Hana Maui, Isabella grapes, peels of raw sugar cane, papayas with unassuming dull yellow skins hiding their sweet-meated interior, and a whole pineapple, hollowed and cored and cut in spears, and then reassembled. Obviously the author was well thought of to be brought such a display of hospitality. Perhaps he was known to love these rich treasures of the islands, for if he had been given such a treat before and had let his hosts know of his delight, the Hawaiians were such people that they would remember, and outdo themselves to offer their guest an even more bountiful display to be enjoyed on his next visit.

She couldn't resist the temptation, and she slid one long cool spear of pineapple from its arrangement, smiling with satisfaction as she ate it hungrily, letting the juice roll down her fingers and onto the towel she and Nicolas Carruthers had played their silly game with just a short time before. She was enjoying herself so much that she gave an almost guilty start when she realized that Carruthers had entered the room and was standing over her, watching the messy operation with a wide smile.

"I see you enjoy some of the pleasures of this paradise where you live."

"I didn't have any lunch, and I hoped you wouldn't mind if I helped myself, Mr. Carruthers."

"Call me Nick, please. I missed lunch, too. As soon as I got here from the airport I ran down for a quick swim, instead." He sat opposite her and began carving a mango with decisive slashes of the fruit knife. "So, let's indulge ourselves in an orgy of sweetness, shall we?"

With that he reached over and popped a piece of mango into her mouth so quickly she didn't have time to object. Then she watched him with fascination as he caught the dripping flavor of the fruit off the knife with his tongue, then dropped a grape or two into his mouth.

He was now wearing a pair of light denim pants and a casual cotton shirt with a faintly Hawaiian motif in its blue design. He had obviously used a dryer on his hair, and the quick process had blown a fullness into the thick dark waves of hair, which he wore longer than most of the men she knew. Being a writer, she supposed he was less bound by the rules of current style than her banker brother-in-law. Even during this short encounter with him, she had already learned that he was a man who probably did exactly as he wanted, without much regard for what appeared right or proper.

A wave of apprehension swept through her as she considered the relationship with him that she had committed herself to. They would have to spend hours together in the days ahead while he interviewed her, those questioning blue eyes studying all her answers, weighing them, separating the truth from the fantasy.

"Would you like a slice of this papaya?" he asked as he halved the luscious fruit that was one of her favorites, spilling its cargo of shiny black seeds onto the tray.

She realized she had been staring at him, lost in solemn thought. "No, thank you. I've had enough," she said, watching him lick the fleshy papaya into his mouth.

For some reason his sensual pleasure in the mere act of eating this snack made her embarrassed to watch him any longer and she jumped up to find her purse on the nearby couch. She was putting a layer of powder over her face when she looked up to see him watching her with a critical squint.

"You shouldn't wear so much makeup," he said suddenly through a mouthful of pineapple.

She swallowed hard, then decided not to reveal her angry feeling that he had no business saying such a thing. With forced calm, she explained that she was sensitive to the sun and wore makeup to protect her fair skin.

"It makes you look older than you are," he said.

To change the subject, Christine walked over to the sliding glass window that looked across the park to the large shape that was visible from all over Waikiki, looking like a crouched lion on lookout toward the sea. It was the famous old dormant volcano named Diamond Head by visiting sailors of the nineteenth century who found glistening volcanic crystals as its base and mistook them for diamonds.

"You can almost see my home from here. I live over there near Diamond Head." She marveled at how, from the viewpoint of this cheerful aerie atop a downtown hotel, the strip of seacoast where she lived seemed menaced by the dominating, rugged, and almost cruel shape of Diamond Head looming over it.

"Your home?"

"Well, not strictly speaking."

"You mean Mrs. Hanover's home, don't you? Where she's lived for thirty years or more?"

"Yes."

"So by your home you really mean a room at your mother-in-law's house, don't you?"

"It's a very nice room," she began lamely, and just then a knock at the door saved her from any further interrogation by this man who was a professional at it and knew just how to get to the most damaging admission in any interview he undertook. If he intended to have her nonplussed and nervous with him before he began their formal discussions, he had already succeeded.

As he walked toward the door she glanced down at the table, where the beautiful display of fruit had been thoroughly ravaged by the two of them. Now the tray contained a slough of stems, seeds, skins, and cores.

"Do you have a kitchenette in this suite?" she called to him. "I think I should clean up this mess before we start our meeting."

"It's right through that door behind you," he called over his shoulder, and Christine quickly carried the remains of their feast into the kitchen and disposed of it while she heard him greet the expected guests. When she came back into the living room, wiping her hands on a kitchen towel, Andrew Hanover and his daughter Jenny were already seated side by side on one of the long sofas.

Obviously surprised to see her coming from the kitchen, Andrew jumped up and came to her.

"Christine, my dear. I didn't realize you were here already. I should have known you wouldn't let us down and be late." Andrew was wearing a three-piece gray suit that was rigidly appropriate to his Ivy League background, however inappropriate it seemed here in Hawaii.

He bent down to kiss her cheek with his dry lips. "What are you doing with that ridiculous rag in your hands? Can't you put it away?"

Christine knew that the heavy sweet smell that still hung in the air should be explained, as well as her uncharacteristic domestic pose with the tea towel as she wiped off the table.

"Nick was nice enough to share his fruit plate with me when I arrived a bit early."

"Nick?" Andrew asked, screwing his face into a painful expression of disapproval. "You mean this famous author, Mr. Carruthers," he corrected her.

Nick placed his hands in his pants pockets, rocked back on his heels, and with a scornful expression said, "After a man and woman have shared a towel, they get on a first name basis real quick. Right, Chris?"

Christine threw the tea towel at him with a boisterousness that brought a surprised lift to Andrew's pale eyebrows. But he could always tell when there was a joke going on that he didn't understand, and he knew better than to try and catch up.

"No one calls my sister-in-law Chris, Mr. Carruthers."

"All right, then. Until she tells me differently, I'll call her Christine, as you do. I'm sure you'll wish me to show your mother the respect of calling her Mrs. Hanover, and now we will be saved the confusion of having two Mrs. Hanovers in our conversations. Now that the first nasty little detail has been resolved, shall we get down to conducting the more challenging negotiations we are her to discuss?"

Andrew Hanover obviously realized that his quarrelsome nature was being made fun of, and that since he was the one who had sought this meeting with the author he had better change his attitude at once to a more welcoming and conciliatory one.

"Of course. Let's sit down and get to it. Christine, you

haven't said hello to your niece," he said, again assuming Christine had forgotten her manners.

Christine stepped over to the double facing couches, stopping to pat the shoulder of the disinterested teenager.

"I'm glad you came along today, Jenny" she said. "I hope you'll take part in this project right along with us."

"I'm supposed to be on vacation," Jenny mumbled in a petulant voice, then looked up at her aunt. "Your hair is all coming loose," she said tartly.

"Oh, yes, so it is," Christine said, nervously patting some silky strands back into the confinement of their hairpins.

Andrew began the discussion. "I've come to know your publisher, John Hicks, quite well when he's been vacationing here in the islands. I've handled some banking problems for him. And he seemed interested when I suggested that an excellent book could be written about the Navy career of my late brother, David Hanover. I was very pleased when he assigned you to the project. I have heard of your reputation for thoroughness, and . . ."

"I wasn't 'assigned' to this project, as you put it," Nick's eyes flashed as he interrupted. "John told me about the idea because he knew that the Navy's Pacific Command has always interested me. This book concept appeals to me because I see it as a way to expand on that theme while perhaps using a central character my readers could identify with."

Realizing he'd made a serious gaffe, Andrew fumbled in his pockets for a package of cigarettes and lit one with hands that shook just a bit.

"Just tell us then how you would like to proceed," he said, expelling the first draft of smoke.

"I would like to interview all of the members of your family, of course. And I want to meet your brother's commanding officers and the men who served under him, especially the ones who were along on that last sea duty. I can't tell you any specific plans for the book until after that."

"I'm sure I speak for my mother when I say that we want to make sure David's heroic nature is fully explored. We are a Navy family, Mr. Carruthers. My father was Admiral

Hanover, and his father and uncle before him both served their country. We want you to describe that continuity of public service, and..."

Christine gave a sideways glance toward the author, having felt a tensing of the man's body even from the other end of the couch she shared with him.

"If you have such specific notions about the book, perhaps you should write it yourself," he said coldly.

"No, no. That's quite impossible," Andrew stammered. "We want a professional job; we want you to do it."

"Then here are my terms. I will write the book based on my own sources of information. And of course you and Mrs. Hanover and Christine will be the key sources of that information. But none of you will have any control over my material, or any editing rights. Do you understand that? No decent journalist would work any other way."

"I didn't mean to suggest that we would interfere. Only that we might make suggestions as to interpretation."

"Your suggestions will be gratefully received," Nick said, easing himself back on the couch so that Christine felt the pillows sag behind her.

"Can we go now?" Jenny said.

"It's too late to do any surfing today. Why are you in such a hurry?" her father asked.

"Some kids are putting together a party tonight, and I promised I'd help."

"You're on vacation, is that what you said?" Nick asked her. Jenny turned to him with obvious relief at being at last able to talk about herself and divert the serious discussion.

"Yes, I'm here to spend the summer with my father. I live in Boston with my mother."

"I'm sure Mr. Carruthers isn't interested in the details of our personal life, Jenny," Andrew said, standing up and pulling the straight legs of his trousers into even more meticulous creases.

"Are you planning to return to Boston to school in the fall?" Nick asked the girl, who now seemed quite interested in the man who was asking her so many questions, sitting up straighter from the slouch she'd been in. "I don't know. I like it here so much I may just stay on indefinitely."

Christine thought she detected a weary sigh from Andrew Hanover at the thought of having his rambunctious daughter as a permanent houseguest in his quiet home in the exclusive Portlock area of Honolulu.

Andrew was fidgeting, anxious to conclude all the arrangements. "How do you wish to start your work, then?" he asked the author.

Christine had a sudden anxious premonition that she was about to be thrust on center stage. Nick Carruthers could interview David's mother, brother, and fellow Navy men for weeks on end, but she knew that she herself was the real key to the man whose character and career he wished to study. She was the one who knew the personal details, who had heard the man's most secret thoughts, who had witnessed daily that obsessiveness required of a man dedicated to duty. She had been David's wife and knew better than anyone the exact nature of his heroism. Since his death two years ago she had kept the memory of that heroism alive, honored him with every act of her busy life. The responsibility of communicating all this to an impersonal listener was overpowering. As she sat overcome by her uncertainties she felt the gaze of the man on the couch beside her turn, just as she'd expected, upon her.

"I'd like to learn about David Hanover's personal life, and the best place to start is with his wife, I think."

So he instinctively knew, as she did, that she held the decoder in her hands.

Andrew came to stand behind the couch, patting his sister-in-law on the head patronizingly. "Christine will be glad to cooperate, won't you dear? You can take a few days to talk to him. Yes, Christine and David had an exceptional marriage. The dashing Navy Commander and his beautiful and admiring wife—they were an inspiration to all who knew them. It was a storybook marriage. I'm sure she can tell you lots of wonderfully happy stories."

"How about tomorrow, then?" Nick asked her.

Christine reached for her purse and took out her appointment book. "Tomorrow? Well, tomorrow is Thursday, isn't it?" She found the page she was looking for. "On Thursday afternoons I always visit David's grave. I also take Mrs. Hanover on Sundays after church; that way we keep fresh flowers there."

"I'll go with you tomorrow. What time should I pick you up?"

"I'm sure you don't want to..." she began.

"I think that's an excellent idea," Andrew said. "The National Memorial Cemetery of the Pacific is a beautiful homage to the heroes of several wars. You can't help but be impressed by it. It's built right on the place the Hawaiians called Puowaina, the hill of sacrifice."

"I'd like to see that; I've never been there," Nick said.

"All right, if you're sure it won't depress you," she said with a sigh. "I have a car, so I'll pick you up in front of the hotel at three o'clock."

With the business settled, they all walked toward the door. Andrew stopped to turn and shake hands with the man he felt he had successfully launched on this project that was so dear to his heart.

"Why don't you plan to return to Mother's house with Christine after your tour tomorrow and we'll all have dinner there together? Mother can meet you, and we can all get to know one another better."

"Fine, I'd like that. See you than. Goodbye, Jenny. I hope you'll be able to join us for dinner."

Jenny was a tiny girl, only a little over five feet tall, and she came over to stand right in front of the tall man who had gone out of his way to be friendly to her. Christine was fairly sure now that Nick was about thirty-five years old, probably twice Jenny's age, but nonetheless she looked up at him with a coquettish smile. "If there isn't a party or something planned that I have to go to, I'll be there."

As Andrew and his daughter left the suite and headed down the hall, Nick grabbed Christine's arm and pulled her back from her intention of following them.

"Aren't you forgetting something?" he asked, his fingers enwrapping the dark fabric of her sleeve with gentle authority, as she heard the elevator grind into place, and her family get into it without her.

"What?" She stared up into the incredible dark blue of his eyes. They reminded her of the sea. Not the warm ocean off of Waikiki Beach, but exotic waters far away from here. The Aegean, perhaps, or the cold North Sea.

"You've left your very important appointment book."

"Oh, yes, I think it's on the coffee table." She felt him slowly unloose his grip on her and she hurried back inside and went over to take the book and stuff it into her purse.

"You say you go to the cemetery every Thursday, and yet you had to consult your little black book in order to remember."

"I'm sort of a forgetful person. Mrs. Hanover gave me this little book, and it helps me to . . ."

"Interesting. You're so scrupulously organized, and yet so easily flustered."

"Until tomorrow, then," she said, anxious to be out from under his perceiving stare.

"Yes, it should be very interesting indeed," he said. "I'm anxious to hear all about that storybook marriage of yours."

The look he gave her was so galvanizing that she felt a tremor go through her entire body. Her reaction was unlike anything she'd ever felt before: a mixture of fear and fascination. She was curious to get to know this man better and find out why he had such an oddly disturbing effect on her nervous system with his insolence. But she dreaded the chinks he might make in her protective armor in the process.

As she squeezed past him in the narrow doorway he said with a lowered voice that sounded incredibly sexy, "I won't see you again until three tomorrow. Unless, of course, you have an attack of the lonelies tonight and want to come back here for more laughs." He leered at her as he tapped on the number on the door. "Remember the place. I'll be here dressed just as you found me."

She reached out and took the door to close it herself in his smirking face. As soon as she was alone in the hallway she leaned back against a wall and closed her eyes tightly for a moment, rubbing at her arm where he'd held onto her. She felt tired beyond her years, and in a moment she began walking dispiritedly toward the elevator at the end of the hall where Andrew and Jenny had disappeared.

So, she was to tell her story to this investigative reporter . . . the romantic tale of a dashing young Navy Commander and his admiring wife. She walked with her usual slow steps, the steps of someone who had nothing to hurry forward to. That's how the world had seen them, she thought. An ideal couple, a perfect marriage, here in this perfect place. Could she keep that myth alive? Or would Nick Carruthers find out that her life with David had been a sham, that she had never had a happy moment with him during her entire marriage?

CHAPTER TWO

WHEN CHRISTINE APPROACHED the hotel at ten minutes before three the next day she laughed out loud to herself, for Nick had anticipated her early arrival and was already waiting. As she guided her car through the traffic she spotted him standing beside the carp pond near the hotel front steps, watching the water with a contemplative look on his face.

Suddenly her eyes played tricks on her. A memory flashed through her brain and she saw him standing as he had yesterday, wrapped only in a towel. She could see the hefty thighs corded with strong muscle, the wide chest where taut skin covered a massive rib cage, and the sheen of tan skin that seemed improbable on the body of a New York writer who has just arrived in Honolulu.

As he got into her car she was still smiling impishly as she enjoyed her secret vision of a strikingly handsome and almost-nude man settling into the seat beside her.

"Is there something wrong with a jeans suit? Am I not suitably dressed for one about to visit the sacred place?" he asked as he noticed the strange look on her face.

"No, you look fine today."

"More respectable than when you first met me, is that it?" he asked her, zeroing in with his usual ability to find the thought behind her words.

"First impressions do tend to linger," she said, trying

hard to repress that first picture of him that stubbornly refused to leave her mind.

As she headed her car up Kapahulu Avenue and onto the Lunalilo Freeway that transversed the busy city of Honolulu, she was aware that Nick Carruthers had turned sideways in his seat and was watching her.

"You aren't dressed as casually as all those gorgeous swinging singles who play around this town, but I'm relieved to find out that at least you don't always dress in black," he said with a slow smile.

This morning she had put on a sleeveless sheath dress of dark blue linen, with tightly stitched tucks down the length of its straight, austere bodice. She knew she did not look like the typical conception of a native islander; in fact, she probably dressed more conservatively than most young women her age on the mainland.

"I'm not here on vacation, you know," she said. "I have responsibilities and duties for which I have to be well dressed."

"Where do you buy your clothes?" he asked.

"Mrs. Hanover has a dressmaker who designs most of our things."

"Just as I thought. Mrs. Hanover wears the widow's weeds and thinks you should remain forever in mourning right along with her," he said. He turned to place a small box he was carrying on the back seat, and noticed a stack of brand new hardbound books resting there.

"You've made a stop at the bookstore today. I'm flattered to see that they carry every one of my titles in print."

"You have obviously spent quite a bit of time here in Hawaii," she said. "The girl at the bookstore said she knows you well, and she keeps your books right out on display."

"Most of my books, as you've probably noticed, have something to do with the countries of the Pacific. So I'm often here on my way to someplace else. I've been thinking of buying a condominium here, as a matter of fact, and setting up a home base. It's far enough from New York to prevent all those interruptions that tend to distract a writer from his work."

Christine was sure that those distractions included a great many female companions. However, if he expected to escape the attention of adoring women, he was coming to the wrong place. An island infested with restless college girls on semester breaks, vacationing divorcees, and working women on holiday certainly ought to provide more then enough diversion for his idle moments.

As the freeway zoomed them over the congested downtown area she wrinkled her nose and said, "You like it here, then?"

"I know it's gotten crowded with the wall-to-wall highrise buildings and the million tourists who pass through each year, but remember, honey, I'm a New Yorker, and I can't live without the excitement and stimulation of a big city around me. Honolulu's got that, plus weather that can't be beat, and rain forests and tropical beaches just minutes away. I'm wild about it; aren't you?"

"Oh, I don't know. It beats Chicago in the winter, I guess."

"You don't sound enthusiastic enough about the place. Don't you realize how most people would envy you your life here?"

"The kind of life I lead could go on in any city or town in the world. I don't have the time to be a perpetual tourist."

"I can tell you don't frequent the beaches."

"How can you tell that?"

"Your skin is so light. You don't have any tan at all."

"I told you, I'm very busy."

"What a shame. You don't even know what you're missing. And your little niece makes a full-time occupation out of going to the beach."

She could tell by the mournful sound of his voice that he indeed felt there was something missing in her life just because she didn't spend all her spare time exploring her adopted homeland. When she had first come here it was as an eager tourist. But within a few weeks she had met David, and since he had lived here most of his life, he wasn't interested in going around to all the local attractions he'd already seen so many times.

Then, after his death it had seemed wrong for her to pursue the gaiety and frivolity of island tourism when her husband had just given his life for his country. And so she went through her daily routines, as she had told him, much as she might in some snowbound city far from here.

"I have a very crowded schedule, what with my volunteer work, and my . . ."

"Reading?" he interrupted, gesturing with one thumb toward his books in the back seat.

"I've always intended to read your books but never got around to it. Now seemed like a logical time."

"The old military technique of 'know your enemy,' is that it?"

"Enemy? Oh, come now. I certainly do not expect to be in the adversary position with you," she said lightly, but she couldn't contain the rising feeling of alarm within her.

"You know, I may ask you some questions you don't like. I think I should warn you of that right now. When you read my books you'll see. I don't settle for clichés and myths; I go after the truth, and sometimes people resent my methods of getting it."

"Why are you telling me this? You just might scare me away from this project."

"You don't seem to me like a lady who scares very easily. I'm telling you because I want you to understand that you mustn't take any of this personally or resent the questions I have to ask you."

Christine tried to concentrate on her driving and not let her interviewer know how much his words had disturbed her. If her first meeting with him hadn't unsettled her enough, certainly this second one was effectively tightening her nerves and making her sick with dread at the thought of the coming days of squirming under the microscope of his intense study.

They had left the freeway and were now following the bumpy road that wound in a slow spiral up and around the outside of the extinct old Punchbowl volcano. At last they came around a curve at the top, and the road became a long double driveway through the huge grassy bowl that had once been the crater of the volcano. The sight was so vividly striking, even to Christine, who came here often, that any further conversation or fearful thoughts were instantly silenced by the majesty of this memorial to some twenty thousand servicemen who had perished in World War II, Korea, Vietnam, or some isolated incident of unexpected violence such as the unfortunate David had encountered in the China Sea just two years ago.

"It was quite beautiful here on Memorial Day," she said to Nick in a hushed voice as they left the car. "The Boy Scouts came and put a cross at every headstone draped with a flowered lei."

That reminded her of the sack she'd brought with her, and she leaned back into the car to find it. Christine had arisen early that morning, as was her routine every Thursday, and gone to the riotously blooming pink plumeria tree in Mrs. Hanover's garden to make a lei for David.

"And you were here on Memorial Day, too, of course," Nick muttered as they started across the close-cropped lawns. There was a brooding note of bitterness to his voice that Christine could not understand. "The dutiful little wind-up toy soldier, reporting for duty to pay her last respects, again and again."

Christine ignored his contemptuous comments—he was obviously not a sentimental person—as she made her way along a familiar route between marble plaques to David's grave. When she had indicated the spot to Nick with a wave of her hand he barely looked at it, turning away slightly, and with politely blank eyes staring off toward the statue at the Court of the Missing across the lawn, giving her some moments of privacy in which to be alone with her thoughts of the past.

She stood in the bright sun holding the sweet-smelling plumeria blossoms close to her face, letting the cloying odor of the flowers carry her on a drift of memories back to her days with David. Her eyes filled with tears as she moved her lips from flower to flower on the endless chain, counting the shattered dreams, the unfulfilled expectations, the thwarted plans that had marked the days of her married life.

She had failed David! How she wished for just one more chance to try to please him. One more opportunity to understand him. Every Thursday her litany was the same. Regrets, and more regrets.

She leaned down and slowly curled the string of flowers around the marble carving of her husband's name on the marker at her feet. As she stood up she saw that Nick had turned and was watching her, his face paled by the bright spotlight of sunshine that focused on them as they stood together in the center of this enormous grassy Punchbowl crater. His eyes narrowed slightly, and she suddenly felt hypocritical beneath his gaze, as she choked back a sob for the man who had been gone from her life for two years, and who had been inaccesible to her for the two years before that when they shared a marriage bed.

Nick assumed she had been a happy wife. But even from his viewpoint her grief probably seemed pathologically intense, or not very believable, she decided. She tried to erase the agony from her face as she began her plodding walk slowly back to the car. Was it the unfinished business between David and herself that kept the wound open and festering for so long, she wondered?

After she'd taken just a few steps she felt Nick come rushing up behind her to grab her hand and twirl her in the opposite direction. Then he began rushing away, pulling her along beside him. His voice boomed out over the deserted area like a loud speaker announcement.

"Come on, girl. Throw those shoulders back and march! Show your pride to the whole world."

"Are you crazy?" she stammered, after trying to shush his loud voice.

"No, I am not crazy. I'm alive, and so are you. And this is the place where you'd better show it."

She looked around her, grateful to see there was no one within earshot.

"Let go of my hand. Have you no respect whatsoever?"

He was still pulling her along after him, his giant strides so quick that she had to almost skip along to keep up with

him or else be in danger of having his crushing clasp on her
hand pull her over onto her face on the ground.

"That's it, let's keep this parade moving, ma'am."

"But you're going the wrong way. The car is back that
way," she gasped.

"I see a lookout spot over on the rim of the crater." He
slowed his pace at last, but ignored her gasping breath
beside him. "I'll bet you never even take the time to come
over here and enjoy the view."

He was leading her up some steps to a platform that
looked out over the entire city, from Diamond Head to the
Waianaes. The view was magnificent. The two of them
were alone, so she could tip her body back and forth with
a great show of suffering as she tried to restore her normal
breathing.

"What if someone had seen us? You can't act that way
here!" she gasped between breaths.

"I can't stand to see you looking so forlorn. I think that
when you're here you should act proud, rather than defeated.
You made the most noble sacrifice a woman can make. You
gave your husband to the cause. You have no reason to act
ashamed and guilty."

"I am not ashamed of anything. And what could I possibly feel guilty about?"

"You tell me. You were the one who was crying. And
the funeral is long since over."

She reached up quickly to brush the last remnants of a
tear away from where it stuck to one long eyelash. She
turned her attention to the view and tried to concentrate on
picking out landmarks she knew. From here, at the rim of
the crater, she could see what Nick meant about the contrast
of urban sprawl surrounded by lush valleys or intense green
tropical vegetation. Perhaps this place did contain the best
of two distinctly different worlds.

"I've brought you a gift," Nick said in a voice gentler
now than it had been moments before.

"A gift? This is hardly the proper time or place for gift
giving."

"Oh? Why is that?" He handed her the box that she'd

seen him put in the back seat of the car. She had assumed he was going to honor her husband's grave with flowers too, and that by now the box was empty.

"Do you think me an iconoclast simply because I venerate the living?" he asked, watching her face.

She opened the box and saw nestled inside an elaborate lei of white carnations interspersed by bright purple splashes of vanda orchids. This was the expensive work of one of Honolulu's top florists, not something handmade by a penitent widow from garden flowers.

"Why, it's wonderful," she murmured, lifting it out of the box. She loved the spicy smell of carnations, and they immediately reminded her of the big vase of flowers her mother kept on the piano in their apartment in Chicago.

"This is for me?" she asked him, beginning to smile.

"Yes, and I expect you to wear it." He took the lei from her hands, placed it around her neck, and then held her by the shoulders and leaned down to kiss her on each cheek in a passionless parody of the dockside ceremonies bestowed on millions of tourists by their island greeters upon their arrival in Honolulu.

"Welcome to the land of the living, little *malihini*," he said softly, rolling the sound of the Hawaiian word with just the proper cadence that she had never been able to imitate.

"I'm not a newcomer. I've been living in Hawaii for almost four years."

"Living? I'm not sure you have ever known a thing about living. And obviously no one has ever taught you."

Christine felt the warm tug of an errant breeze pull at her snug hairdo as if playing with it. It was the northeasterly tradewinds that made the Hawaiian weather so ideal in the summer. Perched here on this spectacular volcano rim, with a view of the entire area that comprised her life, she began to feel lucky indeed. What a beautiful island, surrounded by thousands of miles of sea, inhabited by happy people, warmed so constantly by the sun. Perhaps she should take more time to learn about what it had to offer.

She was reluctant to leave this new viewpoint of the

place she had taken for granted for so long, but Nick had taken her hand and was leading her away from the view and back toward the car. She reached up to remove the lei, intending to leave it behind at the memorial to the missing in action.

"No, you put that back on," Nick reprimanded her, a cloudy look obscuring his usually clear blue eyes. "I didn't buy those flowers just to have them die abandoned in the hot sun. I bought them for a real, live flesh-and-blood girl to enjoy."

"But they are so beautiful. They should be left to honor heroes."

"I intended them as a tribute to you. I thought you understood that. I will be very offended if you don't wear them."

"What will Mrs. Hanover think when I come in all decorated like this?"

"Tell her you've been given an award for your loyalty, your martyrdom. She'll like that. But I want you to understand they are a tribute to your youth and your beauty. Flowers are meant for the living."

Christine knew that she would never again fashion a lei on Thursday morning without wearing it around her own neck before bringing it to David. This unconventional man was already changing her views on things in a very interesting way. Interesting, but also disturbing. Christine's life had been comfortable so far, and simple in its changeless and certain routine. No thinking was required, no changing of attitudes, or freshening of opinions. Only constant and vigilant devotion to the dead hero, and endless hours of remorse.

But now Christine felt disturbing quakes in her sad serenity, tiny warning eruptions that brought hot lava flowing to the surface of the smoldering mountain of her emotions. Warnings she knew she should pay more attention to as she kept her hand secure within Nick's and they quick-stepped together back to the car.

"We'd better hurry. Mrs. Hanover always has cocktails at exactly six o'clock," Christine warned as she parked her

car in the circular driveway in front of the stone steps to
the Hanover house on Diamond Head Road. Nick ducked
his head to avoid several of the large hanging pots of fern
that hung on the wide porch surrounding the house.

"I hope these aren't man-eating plants," he laughed, for
indeed the effect was quite sinister, with the foliage shading
the porch so that little sunlight made its way into the house.

In answer to Christine's ring, Mrs. Wang opened the
door for them, and since Christine had an expected visitor
with her, led them with bowing ceremony down the long
front hall and into the living room.

Nick kept pausing on the way to look at the family portraits: all stern-faced men in military uniforms. Christine
had to turn around to pull him away from the last painting
in the line. It was a study of David, with a bronze plaque
beneath his name saying "KIA," meaning he had the more
exalted honor than the others of having been killed in military action. And the prominent position of his portrait, right
outside the mahogany double doors into the living room,
made his celebrity status in the family history evident.

Mrs. Wang was opening the doors for them as Christine
tugged at Nick's sleeve to come along. He responded by
leaning down to whisper in her ear, "I feel as though I'm
about to have an audience with the queen. It it true they
wear nothing at all beneath those ermine robes?"

Christine couldn't contain the explosion of laughter that
his effrontery provoked. As she stepped inside the room the
joyous echo of her laugh resounded from every corner of
the dour room, lighting it up with a mirth that rarely illu-
minated its shadowy corners.

"Christine, you know that Mother does not like loud
noises in the house. Certainly you can see that such a raucous
outburst might disturb her."

Christine sighed, swallowing the laugh, and walked over
to the man standing in the middle of the room with a cigarette
between his lips.

"Good evening, Andrew." Then she turned to bow
slightly in the direction of a large upholstered chair. Her
eyes had not yet adjusted to the dimness of this room where

the drapes were always kept closed, keeping any natural light out. "Mrs. Hanover, good evening."

"Dear child, you certainly seem exuberant this evening," came a voice from the depths of the wingback chair. Introduce our guest to me, and then come and explain what you're doing with that horseshoe of flowers around your neck."

Christine quickly removed the carnation lei she was still wearing and placed it on a nearby table, and hurried like a dutiful child to do as her mother-in-law bid.

"Mrs. Hanover, I'd like to present Nicolas Carruthers, the writer who will be doing the book about David."

"Come over here, young man, where I can take a closer look at you."

Nicolas strode across the room, and reached for a table lamp near Mrs. Hanover and switched it on.

"Perhaps with a little more light you can assess me better, Mrs. Hanover."

Mrs. Hanover leaned forward into the circle of light and there was a hush of expectation in the room. She had the refined appearance of an aging aristocrat, but beneath her graying hair and pampered soft-skinned face, it was plain to see that a stubborn and regal will power strengthened her.

"Are you so sure that one look at your handsome face will reassure me as to your writing abilities?" she jousted back at him, and Nick gave a good-natured laugh that indicated he found her a delightful sparring partner, and he pulled a chair up close to her and the two of them began to chat.

"Let me fix you a drink, Christine," Andrew said, speaking close to her ear. "Come over here to the bar with me," he added conspiratorially.

In one corner of the room there was an intricately carved liquor cabinet that Mrs. Hanover and her late husband had had custom-made for them on one of their duties in the Orient. Andrew had opened it and was mixing the customary gin and tonics for his family, and a scotch and water that Nick had requested of him.

"Christine, you seem to be treating your work with Mr. Carruthers as if it were some kind of a lark, giggling about like a schoolgirl. I assure you, you have responsibilities to the family that you had better keep in mind."

"What do you mean, Andrew?"

"I mean this. Mr. Carruthers has chosen to start this project with you, and you will be feeding him information just when he is deciding about the project, and formulating his ideas. You must keep him interested in the project, and make sure he takes the viewpoint we expect."

"Now how can I do that?" she asked with a very real feeling of helplessness.

Andrew handed her a drink, and interrupted their conversation to take glasses over to the twosome chatting together across the room. When he came back his brow was furrowed and he seemed paler than ever beneath his thatch of blond hair turning silvery with middle age.

"You're an intelligent girl. I'm sure you can provide him with the necessary information, convince him that our family heritage is important to us. Just keep your wits about you, and think before you speak."

"Of course I will do that. There's nothing to worry about. I'm sure Mr. Carruthers won't try to trick us."

"Sometimes these writers get crazy ideas, that's all," Andrew fussed, holding his cigarette in his mouth as he held his drink in one hand and took Christine's elbow to guide her to a couch with the other.

"Now that I've met him I'm wondering if he's respectful enough of authority to handle this material correctly." His eyes were squinted from the smoke wafting into them, which gave him an almost menacing look of authority when he added, "We're counting on you, Christine."

She felt a stab of guilt as she thought of the secret that lay buried in her breast while she was giving Andrew assurances that they had nothing to worry about from Mr. Carruthers. The writer had a perceptive nature, with an uncanny ability to put himself into Christine's mind. He had, as well, the ability to lure her into relaxed and carefree moments where the danger of inadvertently spilling out the truth was especially threatening. She knew she would have to keep her mind on her assignment in the days ahead. She would have to concentrate on portraying her marriage to David Hanover as one of serenity and fulfillment, deeply satisfying to both of them, and as ideal as the family tried to portray it.

As she swished the ice in her glass absently and considered the enormity of the deception she must try to perform upon the experienced writer, she looked up and saw him staring at her from his seat beside Mrs. Hanover. He had been studying her through the gloom, and as she caught his eye she thought she saw there a trace of suspicion, just a bit of doubt, her first hint that Mr. Carruthers was already aware that there were private thoughts locked in her heart, secrets he would use any means necessary to pry loose. She shuddered.

"You weren't paying attention, Christine." Mrs. Hanover often treated her as if she were the schoolgirl member of this household. "Mr. Carruthers was asking for your services as a tour guide during his visit."

"What do you mean?" She stared at him incredulously.

"You've lived in Honolulu for so long, and I'm new here, so I thought that perhaps you would take me around and show me all the tourist attractions," he said, his large blue eyes opened wide with pretended innocence. He was playing a trick on the Hanovers, one that only Christine could see through. "It would make our work together more pleasant, don't you think?"

She knew that he was toying with her, purposely teasing her, for he had already revealed a long acquaintanceship with these islands, and knew more about the popular entertainment haunts of her city than she did.

"You could show me the beaches and the restaurants and the natural attractions, and that way all our long interview sessions wouldn't be so boring for you."

If Christine hadn't known him better, she would have sworn he was flirting with her in this silly game he was playing, and her mouth curved into an unconscious smile as she noticed how earnestly the Hanovers were considering his comments.

"We have some books in our library you might enjoy too, Mr. Carruthers," Mrs. Hanover said, trying to help.

"But I think the best way to learn about Hawaii is to experience it all with a native." He smiled at Christine with a tricky look that indicated he was enjoying his deception thoroughly. He seemed to be planning more a vacation than a work schedule and he intended to take her to these beaches and restaurants and natural wonders with the full knowledge and agreement of those she had told him were her careful chaperones and protectors.

"Mr. Carruthers, though I happen to live in a tourist paradise I do not dance the hula, go to luaus, ride on surfboards, or wear a muu-muu," she said, standing up to face him defiantly. She wanted to make it clear to him that she understood he was making fun of her, tempting her right beneath the noses of the Hanovers, trying to attract her to the world of sun-filled days and balmy nights that went on outside the grounds of this walled estate.

"Then why live in Hawaii?" he drawled. "Come with me and for once let yourself have some of the rewards this place has to offer."

Christine flushed deeply beneath the startled looks of her brother-in-law and his mother. Andrew was obviously displeased that Christine was not being more hospitable in agreeing to the writer's every suggestion. He expected her to win him over to firm allegiance to the family's side during the days ahead, and any sign of crossed wires obviously disturbed him. He ground out his cigarette vigorously as an inspired idea came to him.

"This Saturday night there is a perfect opportunity for Christine to introduce you to our Navy world, Mr. Carruthers. There's to be a fleet party at the Royal Hawaiian Hotel."

"You were going to escort Christine to that party," Mrs. Hanover reminded her son.

"I insist that Nick, here, go in my place. He can't help but be swept up by the patriotism of that event. And when he sees the respect with which Christine is received he'll get a real sense of David's high position in the honorable list of Navy men."

"That's settled, then," Mrs. Hanover said, rising to her feet to take Nick's arm. "Shall we go in to dinner? Andrew, take Christine to the table."

"Isn't Jenny going to join us, Mr. Hanover?" Nick asked.

"I'm afraid Jenny was really quite torn between the idea of dinner with a famous author and a party with six beach boys from Waikiki. It seems the beach boys have won out."

Amid polite laughter they began a stately procession to the dining room, accompanied by Andrew's forced social patter about the state of the weather that day and what could be expected the next. Because her mind always wandered when he was speaking, Christine overheard the brisk commands Mrs. Hanover was giving to her dinner partner as that couple walked in front of her. The planked floor almost fell away from beneath her feet with shock when she heard the words, "You'll move into my house for the duration of your stay in Honolulu, Mr. Carruthers. That will make your work easier and more pleasant, I think."

Christine knew that was the Hanover way of keeping an eye on people.

The next day was a rare one, when Christine had hours of free time to herself. Usually she and Mrs. Hanover had their standing appointments with the hairdresser on Friday mornings, but Christine's had been postponed until Saturday because of the formal dance she would be attending that night.

So, with rare capriciousness, she took one of Nick's books and went to spend the morning on the beach below the Hanover estate. It was almost noon when she came up the long stairway into the gardens behind the house, her fair skin glistening from the thick layer of coconut-scented sun cream she had applied to protect her seldom-exposed skin. She was lost in thought, slowly trudging up the path that led between blooming hibiscus bushes and the velvety leaves of dark green banana plants, oblivious to their beauty.

When she came to a widening in the path where a group of garden chairs invited a resting place, she put her beach bag down on one chair, and then sat down on another facing it, staring into space with such concentration that it appeared as if she were listening to the voice of someone who wasn't there.

Then a very real voice announced from behind her, "Well, look at the native beauty I've found in the garden of my new home. My hostess thinks of everything, doesn't she, providing for my every comfort this way?"

Nick leaned over the chair from behind her, placed both hands on her shoulders, and whispered into her ear as if the foliage around them might be eavesdropping.

"Tell me, my sweet, do your services come with the use of the room?"

His voice was husky, and his innuendo made Christine feel an unwelcome surge of excitement. As his hands on her bare shoulders began to feel more caressing than friendly, she stood up to escape his touch. Then, facing him, she felt one of her blushes begin to creep over her, this one starting clear down at her ankles and traveling with a hot rush upward to the base of her neck.

She had forgotten how scantily she was dressed. She had on a black two-piece bathing suit with strings on each hip that made it possible to draw up the fabric into a daring bikini. She was grateful she was wearing the suit with as much coverage as possible, the string ties demurely fastened into small bows. But the top of the bathing suit was inadequate to contain the bosomy white flesh that overflowed its neat triangles, and that area of her body seemed to attract Nick's immediate attention.

"If you're going to start working on a tan, you'd better take it easy. I see a pink flush that just might be the start of a bad sunburn."

She lunged for her tote bag nearby and pulled at the edge of her beach robe bunched down inside. However, she succeeded only in dislodging her bottle of suntan lotion and Nick swooped down and grabbed it, then took a position in front of her so that she couldn't reach the safety of her robe.

"Turn around," he commanded. "Let's start with your back." And he began slowly massaging the creamy lotion where the light touch of his hands had already awakened her sensitivity.

"I didn't know you would be moving in here so soon," she said haltingly, trying to keep her mind off of the intimate movement of his fingers across her shoulders and back. She certainly would never have walked about the grounds without her robe over the bathing suit if she had suspected she might encounter him. She had become used to feeling hidden away here on the secluded Hanover estate.

"I couldn't stay away from you another minute," he said, mocking her with a lusty passion to his voice. "I've come to live with you and make you happy," he said, this time going too far.

"Now stop that. If Mrs. Hanover ever heard how you talk to me she'd boot you right out her front door."

"I'm sorry. I forgot my place. I forgot I was speaking to the untouchable Hanover widow."

She let him go on with what he was doing, happy at least to have her back to him so that he couldn't continue his study of her voluptuous shapeliness.

"What were you doing when I came upon you? You looked as though you were talking to a ghost," he said.

Her mood took a sudden nosedive into despondency, and her voice was small and quiet when she answered him. "This is where David and I used to come to talk sometimes, when we needed privacy. Maybe I was sort of listening to a voice from the past."

His attitude immediately became more serious as he tightened his grip on her enough to spin her around to face him.

"Do you mean to say that you and David never had a home of your own? You lived here with his mama?"

"He was away on sea duty a lot of the time. It seemed like the most sensible thing to do. He didn't want to leave me alone."

"But when he was home with you it was always here in this house."

Now that she saw Nick's eyes flash with such outrage, the idea did seem less reasonable than it had when David had insisted upon it. But she quickly remembered the concept of perfection she must maintain concerning her marriage.

"Can you think of a more beautiful setting? This romantic garden, our lovely suite of rooms. We were very happy here," she said, congratulating herself on not stumbling on a single word. "It's certainly better than the officers' housing at Little Makalapa."

"Have you ever lived on your own, then?"

"No, I lived with my mother in Chicago after my father died. That was while I was going to nursing school. Then she was killed in an accident, and shortly afterward I came to Hawaii on a vacation and met David. We had what they call a whirlwind courtship and we were married right away."

"Love at first sight, whirlwind courtship, storybook marriage. Yes, yes, I've heard all about it. And then here you were, right back living with mother again."

She stared into his eyes, trying to determine how much of what he said was in jest, and how much he was really able to sense about the search for security and stability that had motivated her life in the past. But she realized too late that it was not wise to expose herself to the power of those deep sea blue eyes of his. They sent her messages so heavily laden with empathy and understanding that she felt herself fall slack as if mesmerized before him.

"What a poor little overprotected girl you are. Keeping yourself walled up so safely, devoting yourself to the past, you're so afraid of the unknown, of the future. Don't you believe in taking any chances?"

He had taken up both her hands in his, and was holding her at arm's length, studying her as he said this. But then he ever so slowly began to slip his hands up her arms, bringing her closer and closer to him. She felt her breath catch in warning, and her eyelids fluttered as fast as a butterfly's wings. There was something so captivating about

Nick's physical nearness that she was terrified of succumbing to it.

She knew that he was going to take her into his arms for an embrace, and with her last shred of resistance she darted a quick look around to see if they were adequately hidden by the thick foliage.

And then he kissed her, rather calmly, almost as if he meant to soothe her with his sympathy. But the effect on her was shattering, and she knew she had to make him stop before he broke through her fragile control.

"Please don't do that," she said, pulling away. "Someone might see you from the house."

He released her at once. "How polite you are, Mrs. Hanover. Saying 'please' and all. I will respect your wishes, but only because I so enjoy my duties anointing the sacred maiden."

Before she could stop him he had untied the strings at her hips and with a quick pull on each side had drawn up her suit into the fetching bikini shape she avoided.

"You should be sunning in the nude for a perfect tan, but since I'm sure you'd be offended at the idea, at least reveal as much skin as you can."

His wandering fingers now began to find new places to apply the cream, exploring her thighs and then moving up to her taut stomach as she stood before him, numbed by the unknown luxury of a man's attentive devotion to her.

"Gorgeous, absolutely gorgeous," she heard Nick mumbling under his breath.

"What did you say?"

"You have one gorgeous body, lady, and I think what makes it so enticing is the fact that you aren't even aware of what a bombshell you are."

"Oh, please!" she said with a modest little laugh.

"Don't you know what a body like this does to a man? This spot right here could send my mind reeling. And this part is so perfect it could make a slave of any man who sees it. And this, and this . . ."

Christine was not sure if he was making fun of her, or truly admiring her figure with his ridiculous commentary

as he spread the white film over every part of her body he
could reach.

"The smell of this coconut lotion just may be a powerful
aphrodisiac," he laughed. "You smell like those chi chis
they serve in a pineapple shell at Don the Beachcomber's."

His hands were now stroking upward on her neck, slath-
ering the sweet smell of coconuts so near her face that she
couldn't escape its stupefying effect, and then he stopped
when he came to her chin, and pulled her face toward him.

"And I love chi chis," he whispered, kissing her lightly.
"In fact, I can't get enough of them."

"Mmm," she murmured. "They sound good. I've never
had one. I must try one sometime."

He kissed her again. "Mmm. Yes, you must. Or a piña
colada."

She reached up to place her hands around his neck. "I
love the taste of coconut."

"Is that what I'm tasting that I like so much? I thought
it was you."

When he kissed her this time the calmness that had held
him in check the first time was absent. He seemed as over-
powered as she was. He let his hands slip over her oily
body, twisting her about in his arms so that she felt every
variety of sensation he had to offer her with his embrace.
His touch slid up her backbone to the nape of her neck, then
back down to the base of her spine where his large hands
completely covered the small space of the bikini bottom,
urgently pressing her toward him, tilting the lower half of
her body so that she could not miss the thrilling throb of
his desire for her.

His mouth against hers was just as reluctant to be still
as his hands. His kiss was urgent and exploratory, and
brought alive in Christine sensations she had never known
before. She had never felt such unbridled and tumultuous
passion, never known the insatiable hunger for more that
a man could arouse with such skilled attention to what might
please her. He had flattered her with his teasing worship
of her body, giving her the subtle suspicion that she just
might be a sexually magnetic person. Then the slow sen-

suousness of the massage had further prepared her, without her even realizing it. It had stoked a slowly growing fire until it erupted into this fiery heat that she now welcomed with exultant thrusts of her body against his.

The new sensations coursing through her body blocked out all the nagging thoughts and worrisome problems that would soon clamor for her attention. Lying on the beach today she'd read several chapters from one of Nick's books, and what she had read frightened and dismayed her. She learned from his own pages that he was a man not to be trusted, a dangerous opponent in a game she was not properly prepared to play. She had promised herself to be careful; she would plan her every move, she would never let down her guard. She had sat here alone in the garden reviewing moments of her life with David that had been so savagely destructive she knew she must at all costs keep them hidden from her ruthless adversary, just as she'd kept them buried from the world and from herself.

And here she was, just moments later, writhing in his arms, holding back moans of pleasure with the greatest difficulty, her heart taking happy, perilous leaps about inside her soul.

"I can't wait until tomorrow night," he said with obvious difficulty as he drew himself away from her, shaking his head slightly as if to clear his thinking.

"Why, what's tomorrow night?" she asked stupidly.

He touched her trembling lips with one finger in a brief salute of farewell, then made a slow turn and began to walk away from her, back toward the house. "Have you forgotten? Tomorrow night you and I are going out on our first date."

CHAPTER THREE

"WHERE IS MRS. HANOVER? I want to talk to her right away," Christine said as soon as she came in the front door after parking her car. There was fire in her eyes, and she was ready to do battle, but when Mrs. Wang informed her that her mother-in-law wouldn't be downstairs until six o'clock she took a deep calming breath and decided she would have to sustain her outrage a bit longer and go upstairs and get dressed for the fleet party.

As she headed upstairs and stripped to get into the shower she thought about the books she had taken with her to the hairdresser's this afternoon. The reading she'd done while under the dryer had served to amplify what she'd found out when she began her reading on the beach yesterday of the complete works of Nicolas Carruthers. Every one of his books was sensational in its revelations of some previously unperceived problem or social dilemma. No wonder the books were such best sellers! He specialized in startling and unexpected surprise twists, and his approach was always that of a tenacious reporter, sleuthing out hidden facts.

As she toweled herself dry she worriedly considered what kind of a book he might write about David. Did he plan the glorifying description of a saintly martyr that Mrs. Hanover and Andrew had foreseen? Obviously not; who would buy that? He wanted to write a book that would attract attention, sell copies, and keep the money rolling in to support his luxurious world travels.

While reading the books she had resolved to come home and confront Mrs. Hanover at once with what she'd learned. She planned to warn the woman that she may have invited a traitor into their lives, to live right amongst them while he gathered whatever scurrilous information he might be able to use to make fools of them. If she hurried downstairs as soon as she was dressed she could catch her mother-in-law for some private moments of discussion before the intrusive houseguest put in his appearance.

After the hot shower and the brisk rub-down with the towel, Christine felt more stimulated by her anger than ever, and she flung herself nude across her bed for a few moments of rest. When she got up her breathing had returned to normal and some of her composure had returned; she began to dress.

She stood for some moments before the mirrored door of her dressing room, staring at herself. Dressed in only her bra and bikini panties she looked very much the way she had yesterday in her two-piece suit when she had unexpectedly been confronted by Nick in the garden. She ran her fingers up her arms, regarding with wonder the body that had caused such an explosive reaction to its beholder. Could it be that she really was a beautiful woman, with a body capable of attraction?

She tried to remember her husband David's reactions to her. He always seemed to take her figure for granted, even indicating he preferred a more slender woman, and suggesting now and then that she go on a diet. Those vague hints of disapproval had been enough to make her doubt her sexual drawing power. But now Nick Carruthers acted toward her as if she were a powerful magnet, unleashing his most primitive instincts for possession. He had flirted with her at their first meeting, presented her with a gift on their second meeting, and kissed her so passionately on their third meeting that she was still reeling a day later from the effect.

She knew that tonight, accompanying him to this formal dance, she would have to be particularly careful, for he was

the last man in the world she wanted to form any relationship
with. She had to remain on guard against his assaults, both
physical and mental. She had to have her defenses ready.
She had practiced rigid self-control for years; there should
be no problem in wearing the familiar mask that concealed
her emotions.

She reached into her long wardrobe and ran her fingers
down the row of formal gowns. She had at least a half-
dozen of them, because she often accompanied Mrs. Hanover or Andrew to some military party or civic function.
They were all the type of dresses sold in stores as "mother
of the bride" gowns, with long sleeves and high necks meant
to cover the symptoms of aging in the matrons who usually
bought them. In Christine's case, the gowns were meant to
conceal from everyone, including herself, the youthful al-
lure her figure was capable of conveying.

She pulled out a beige chiffon. It had a cowl neck, and
from there fell straight to the floor in a swirl of gauzy
sheerness. Any seductive qualities the dress might have had
were eliminated by the matching taffeta slip designed to be
worn under the dress. As she slipped it on she was grateful
for its chaste simplicity, smiling to herself as she realized
no man could be excited by her appearance tonight, even
Nick Carruthers.

She walked slowly down the stairs and toward the living
room, hating the bad news she was bearing, but hoping that
Mrs. Hanover would accept her warning and put Mr. Carruthers out of their lives, bag and baggage. When she opened
the doors, she was surprised to see Nick seated across from
Mrs. Hanover's usual chair. They were having a drink together like old friends.

Her plan foiled, she stood flustered by the door, wondering if there was any way left to get out of spending the
evening with a man she knew to be a spy. How could she
endure the next few hours until she had the opportunity to
tell Andrew or his mother what she suspected and have them
eject Nick from this house? Then she saw him walking
toward her, his eyes sparkling with a love of combat that
seemed, again, to indicate he knew what she was thinking.

"I know this is more a business meeting than a date," he said for Mrs. Hanover's benefit, giving Christine a wicked and discreet wink. "But being the gallant type, I brought you a little something, anyway."

He walked toward her and handed her a florist's box. He was wearing a white dinner jacket that made him appear even more stunningly virile than ever, the light coat providing a dramatic contrast to his wavy dark hair, the dark pants accentuating the lean length of his legs.

Inside the box was one perfect white gardenia, affixed to a comb so that it could be worn in the hair.

"I've never seen such a large gardenia. Why, it's beautiful," she said, removing it from the box and hurrying toward the mirror over a credenza in the corner of the room.

"You must leave Mr. Carruther's kind gift here in a bowl of water to appreciate when you come home, dear," Mrs. Hanover called from the murky depths of her chair. "It would not look appropriate for you to wear it."

"But it's made to be worn in the hair," she said, hesitating.

"I am not taking a Honolulu resident to a party without a flower behind her ear," Nick said so forcefully that even Mrs. Hanover was stilled.

Soon she had fastened the flower in place amid the tightly arranged and lacquered curls the hairdresser had piled on her head like a crown. Nick came to her side, took her arm with studied gentlemanliness, and guided her toward the door, giving a low growl that only she could hear and saying, "The white of that flower makes your new tan really glow."

He looked rather like the cat who had eaten the canary, she thought, marveling at how much fun he was having playing the dual roles of trusted family friend and deceiving seducer.

From the doorway he turned to give a pious assurance to his hostess. "Since you've entrusted me with this precious lady, I vow to protect her with my very life," he joked. "And to bring her home safely."

"See that you do that, Mr. Carruthers. My son's wife is very dear to me," Mrs. Hanover replied, getting up to watch the two of them with an unexplainably rapt expression as they exited into the hall. She seemed to have put a special emphasis on the word "wife," as if to remind Nick to watch his manners, that his conduct in this area, at least, was being watched.

Christine wished that her mother-in-law could know the full treachery of the man she'd been assigned to spend the evening with. If only she had come downstairs early enough to catch Mrs. Hanover alone, she could have told her Nick's plans to extract information from them for his book. But Nick was already so used to her habit of being early that he'd beaten her down the stairs; now she would have to endure this long evening, postponing her startling revelations for Mrs. Hanover until tomorrow.

They pulled up in front of the pinkish stucco Moorish castle that was the oldest luxury hotel in Honolulu—the famous old Royal Hawaiian. Nick had insisted on driving her car, telling her that he had a sportier model of the Mercedes at home in New York, so he was familiar with it; now he turned the car over to the parking attendant and ushered her through the corridors toward the Monarch Room as if he knew right where it was.

They were surrounded on all sides by arriving military brass, all dressed in their beautiful "mess dress"—dark blue pants, short white jackets, and gold cummerbunds. Christine had always loved formal Navy parties. It was like stepping back in time to a more elegant era, and though Nick wasn't officially a part of the Navy world, tonight he seemed to fit right into the mode of tall, active men, confident and proud to be seen wearing their most flattering attire.

"We're going to sit with our ship tonight," Christine informed Nick as soon as they entered the huge and famous old dining room.

"Sit with our ship? Now what does that mean, old salt? You'll have to translate your Navy lingo for me."

"That means we will be at a table reserved for the officers of David's destroyer. I think you'll like that; you said you wanted to meet the men he worked with."

"Oh, fine. This is the one night you've consented to go

out with me for wild, uninhibited fun, and now you've got me working already." He pretended to complain, but Christine was sure that she could see him mentally sharpening a pencil and finding clean new pages in an imaginary notepad where he could take down every surprising fact he could gather up tonight. She resolved not to let slip any comments that would be eligible for his dirty little notebook.

"Here's our table," she said.

"There's no one here; they must all be dancing. Shall we join them?" Nick said, taking her purse from her and placing it on the table.

As soon as they were on the crowded dance floor together, she knew she'd made a mistake, for Nick did not settle for the dignified mechanical-man style of dancing most men used with her. She wondered nervously if those who knew her were watching this casually possessive display of intimacy on Nick's part. He pulled her so tightly close to him that she could feel the heat of his body down the entire length of hers, and she knew that his face was pressed close to her hair when he said, "That gardenia smells almost as good as the coconut oil you used on yourself yesterday to entice me."

She pulled back from him abruptly. "I did not in any way try to entice you yesterday, and since you brought it up, I'd like you to know I did not appreciate what happened. I do not want you taking such liberties with me ever again."

"Say please," he teased her, catching her by surprise. For he was acting meekly cooperative, as if her every wish was his command.

"*Please* do not kiss me ever again. If we are to work together you must keep your distance, or I will simply refuse to see you."

"Okay."

"Okay?" She felt an odd tinge of disappointment at his ready agreement to her demands.

"Yes, okay," he said tugging her closer into his arms again. "But don't look so crestfallen. I lie."

"Oh, you!" She laughed in spite of her efforts to repress any such spontaneous reactions to him, and let him twirl her around the dance floor until the chiffon of her layered skirt whirled like a misty cloud around their feet.

At least she was properly forewarned. She had read his books and knew his writing style. And he himself had cheerfully admitted to being a liar. He would probably do much more than that in order to get what he needed for one of his profitable best sellers: steal, cheat, lure. Yes, his ardent attentions to her were probably part of his plan. He saw her as a plain and unloved widow, starved for male attention, a woman who would readily respond to his ardorous flattery and cynical kisses. He had picked her first in the family to work his wiles on, and why not? She was easy to win over, and once she was wooed to his side, the rest of the family would trust him and then provide him with access to all their friends and Navy contacts until he had the inside material he needed. Then he would disappear back to New York, to stab them all with every word he wrote.

Christine could feel Nick's uneven breathing on her cheek and then through the loose chiffon at her neck. At that moment she hated her loneliness and her self-pity for making her so vulnerable. His very closeness, the warmth of his breath—so male, so bracing—were causing reactions in her she wished she could deny. But the disturbance within her was strangely pleasant as well as chaotic.

"If you don't mind, I've had enough dancing," she said crossly, and pushed herself out of his arms.

As he followed her toward their table he leaned forward and admonished her, "Loosen up, lady, you're here to have some fun, remember? It's not a crime to enjoy yourself a little."

Then Christine did loosen up, but the happy sight that prompted her to smile with relief was the sight of her best friend, Kim Malone, and her husband, Peter, heading for the dance floor.

"If you want to find out what I really enjoy in life," she said quickly to Nick, "come and meet my boss lady and hear about our work at NASAP."

"What," Nick gasped in surprise, "is a Naysap?"

"Kim, I didn't know you'd be here tonight," Christine said as the couple came toward them.

"Peter just got back from Okinawa yesterday, so we decided to step out and enjoy ourselves."

"Kim and Peter Malone, I'd like you to meet Nicolas Carruthers, a writer friend of Andrew's who is doing some research here in the islands. Nick, Kim is the Navy's liaison officer for NASAP at Pearl Harbor."

"I repeat the question: what kind of creature from outer space is a Naysap?"

Christine smiled, then hurried to explain proudly, "NA-SAP stands for Navy Alcohol Safety Action Program, and it's just about the most exciting new alcoholism prevention program in the country."

Kim looked at her friend with a fond smile. "Aren't I lucky, Mr. Carruthers, to have such a loyal and enthusiastic woman working for me?"

Nick said to Christine, "Since I've been here you've never mentioned going to work. I didn't know you had a job."

"Oh, I'm only a part-time volunteer, so I can set my own hours."

"I could use Christine forty hours a week or more, if she didn't have to spend so much time holding Mrs. Hanover's hand," Kim said with a smile that lit up her extraordinary Hawaiian-Japanese-Chinese-Filipino-American face.

"Amen!" said Nick quietly. Kim's outspoken opinion obviously appealed to him, for he began questioning her about the program she was in charge of.

"Our goal is to identify the alcohol abuser in his very earliest stages, at the point he first gets in the slightest bit of trouble due to drinking, and then through education and a program to teach self-awareness, try to get him on the right track. Convince him there is a better way to live."

"Keep him a functioning Navy man, is that it?"

"Our results may be a little self-serving; we save the Navy—and therefore you taxpayers—a great deal of money when we rescue a trained man from a drinking problem."

Christine took over, her eyes alight with excitement. Her

job was the one luxury of emotion she indulged herself in. "But you ought to see the letters Kim gets from men who've gone through the program. She's saving lives, not just money. These men are so grateful to her!"

Peter put his arm around his wife's waist and gave Nick a knowing wink. "These girls could stand around and sell you on NASAP all night, but I'm a man just back from sea duty, and I want to get my arms around my wife, if you'll excuse me."

"Sure, go ahead. Dancing is just civilization's way of allowing a little public groping and grabbing." He turned to Christine. "I could go for a little more of that, couldn't you?" he asked with a suggestive glint in his eye.

"I told you I do not care to dance with you any more," Christine sputtered, and she caught a surprised look from Kim as her husband led her away. Obviously, there would be some questioning from her friend Monday when she arrived at work.

Dinner progressed as usual. There were speeches between each course of the meal. A Squadron Commander wheeled out a giant birthday cake, and some milestone date was commemorated in a ceremony with more speeches, and Christine chatted with the young officer seated to her right, while Nick chatted with a recent Navy bride on his left. Christine was surprised that he wasn't taking a more aggressive attitude in trying to meet and question key people. So far he was simply making party conversation and asking for no introductions to important people.

After the cake had been consumed, and the coffee drunk, Nick summoned a waiter and ordered two Kahlúas over ice for them, without asking her if she wanted an after-dinner drink. Everyone else at their table was up and dancing, so they were left alone to sip their sweet drinks.

"Since you won't dance with me, there's nothing left for me to do except get drunk," he said, staring morosely into his drink. "And I warn you, when I get drunk I put lamp shades on my head and try to teach the band leader how to do his job, and then kiss all the girls in the room, and just generally make an unforgettable scene."

Christine laughed at the ludicrous picture he'd drawn. "I doubt very much if you could ever act the fool," she said. "But, all right, I'll dance with you if you'll keep your distance and pretend to respect my position here."

She stood up with a weary sigh of resignation. Then she saw a couple walking toward their table.

"No, wait. There's Admiral Elliot, someone I'm sure you'll want to meet. David served under him."

"Admiral, how are you this evening?" Christine accepted the white-haired man's friendly kiss on the cheek.

"Just fine, my dear. Say, I haven't seen that fine mother-in-law of yours lately. Tell Florence I asked about her."

"I certainly will, Admiral. I'd like you to meet my escort for this evening. This is Nicolas Carruthers, a writer visiting here from New York."

"How do you do," Nick said. "I'm here to research a book on David Hanover, and I'd like to talk to you about him sometime if I may."

The Admiral looked away, distracted by his interest in what had happened to his dancing partner. The tall, willowy redhead in a clinging satin dress of deep burgundy was leaning away from this conversation, talking to some uniformed men behind the Admiral.

"Linda, pay attention, dear. Say hello to Christine Hanover. You remember her, don't you?"

"Of course," the Admiral's daughter smiled, showing off a set of unbelievably straight, shiny white teeth. "I knew *both* Christine and David very well."

Christine wondered for just a moment if the girl had added special emphasis to David's name when she'd mentioned it, and she noticed that Linda Elliott lowered her eyes as if she couldn't quite meet Christine's absorbed stare after she'd made the comment.

Christine introduced Linda to Nick, and then he tried to recapture the Admiral's interest in the work he was about to undertake. It occurred to Christine that perhaps the Admiral knew of Nick's reputation as a hard-hitting journalist and wanted nothing to do with this project, for he kept looking about the room, showing no interest in the discussion.

Then Linda interjected into the conversation, "I will be glad to be interviewed, Mr. Carruthers. Can you dance and ask questions at the same time?" She held her arms out toward Nick, showing with the tilt of her head how intrigued she was to have a stranger in their midst. Linda knew, and was known by, every Navy man at Pearl Harbor, and was constantly looking for new conquests.

As she pulled Nick away she said to Christine over her shoulder, "I know you don't mind sharing your man," giving each word a knife-sharp twist that evaded her father's absentminded notice. Nick, however, seemed to catch some intimation that interested him, for his nostrils fairly flared with his eagerness to get Linda away to the dance floor where he could question her privately.

It was only when Christine was encased in the stiff grip of Admiral Elliott on the dance floor, his preoccupied stare over her head leaving her alone with her thoughts, that she felt a wave of apprehension. Something about Linda's arrogant—and at the same time guilty—attitude had struck a nerve. She glanced over at the girl curved close to Nick's body, one arm wrapped around his neck, and oddly primitive and elemental warnings sounded through her brain. Old resentments flared into life again; ugly frustrations were resurrected. She danced on automatically, but inside her a deep and fast-moving current was moving a river full of remembrances to the overflowing point.

How could she have forgotten? Why hadn't she remembered until this moment? Those jealous feelings toward Linda had nothing to do with Nick. They were leftover residuals of the past. David Hanover had known Linda very well; too well, in fact, to suit his wife. The red-head had been no friend of Christine's; that's why she still avoided her to this day. But she'd been a very special friend to David. So special that Christine had finally found out about his meetings with her and confronted him. When he had refused to stop seeing Linda, Christine had threatened to leave him, and he had assured her they would talk about it when he returned from his duty. But he never returned from that last fateful mission, and Christine had then stepped into her role as the distraught and devoted widow; the couple's conflicts and quarrels had been forgotten ever since.

Was it possible for the human mind to bury something so hurtful and destructive? Could she really have forgotten, until this moment, that her husband was unfaithful to her, had flaunted it before her, and that she had hated him for it?

Damn him, she thought, cursing not the husband who had wronged her, but the new man in town who wouldn't stand for false idols. He was the one bringing all these old hurts to the surface.

However, the long repression of the truth must have come at great cost to Christine, for now the remembering, the facing up to the time of such tragic unhappiness in her life, almost seemed a relief. She felt her steps lighten a bit, and she seemed to be trying to move a bit faster, a bit more in time to the music, than her partner.

"Now, Mrs. Hanover. Just take it easy. We're not going to a fire, you know. Let's slow down and conserve our strength; it's going to be a long evening."

Admiral Elliott was lumping her right in there with the old folks, she noticed with a flare of anger unusual to her subdued senses. The crepe-draped widow, rocking on the porch of the widows' home, conserving her strength. Conserving it for what?

"You forget, Admiral. I'm the same age as your daughter. I can dance all night and still laugh at the dawn."

Admiral Elliott always seemed to be listening to commands or drum rolls far across the Pacific. He rarely zeroed in his attention on a mere dancing partner. But her words apparently interested him, for he gave her a closer look than usual.

"I'm glad to hear such spunky talk from you, young lady. I've worried about you. It's not right to devote one's whole life to empty hero worship. There are new battles to be waged, always new ones. Life goes on."

"Do you think I've been overemphasizing my widowhood, Admiral?" she asked as she considered the possibility herself.

"You accompany Florence to every official function, to her Navy Relief work, dine out only at the Cannon Club, have no young friends of your own. Yes, to speak frankly, you seem a bit compulsive about your devotion."

"Why, Admiral, you surprise me. With all that's on your mind, you mean you've taken such detailed notice of the daily activities of one widow?"

"Once you've been under my command, I take responsibility for you forever," he chuckled, but she knew there was more truth to his words than he would ever admit.

"Now what's this about this writer chap doing research on your late husband?" the Admiral asked her.

"Mrs. Hanover and her son have asked him to do a book about David's Navy career, his rapid rise in rank, his exceptional command of the *U.S.S. Brewster*, the valorous way he handled that last encounter."

"Young lady, those deeds all quite properly died with the doer. I see no point in dwelling on the past."

"But surely David's exploits could serve as an example to younger men . . ."

"Tell your writer friend to make an appointment with my public information officer. He'll be able to give him the official story of what happened."

"But you were a friend of David's father, and you've known the family for years. Don't you want to add your personal comments to the story?"

But as the Admiral hesitated in giving an answer, the music stopped and they were caught up in a jumble of movement as people returned to their tables or changed partners for the next dance. When the Admiral spotted a crony he wished to talk to, Christine excused herself and headed toward the outdoor veranda off the Monarch Room for some quiet moments alone in which to collect her thoughts.

She felt a jumble of confusing new information crashing about inside her brain and she needed time to assimilate it. The sight of Linda Elliott, and the memories she had jostled loose from their years of being buried, were painful to adjust to. And yet Christine felt the first breath of reality sweep over her world in a long time. Her feet seemed to be touching the earth instead of drifting along on an imaginary cloud.

As she looked out toward Waikiki Beach, and watched the strings of softly colored Japanese lanterns swing about in the evening breeze, she felt someone come up close behind her and put his arms about her waist. She did not jump with fright because she knew at once who it was. With calm control she twisted about in his grasp to face him.

"You will have to let go of me, Nick. This is an official Navy function, and I'm here as an honored guest because of my status as the widow of the captain of a destroyer. It would not be right for me to be seen being nuzzled by some mainland visitor just off the plane."

Nick dropped his hands to his sides. "What a beautifully stated rebuff. I feel that I've just been spurned by a real pro. But you've left a loophole in your argument. Come with me, pretty lady."

He turned quickly and headed for the stairs; almost without realizing what she was doing, Christine followed him down into the lush tropical garden of coco palms for which the hotel was famous. She was hurrying to keep up with his long strides when he stopped abruptly, grabbed her by the shoulders, and pulled her into a darkened corner of the garden where the shimmering fronds of a coconut tree concealed them.

"You are so afraid of what people will think if they see us. You are so protective of your image. But now we are completely alone, in a dark corner where no one can see what we're doing. Now this is a matter between you and me alone."

Even in the darkness she could see the bright flare of desire spring into his eyes, and she could feel his breath hot on her cheek. She felt the panic of being trapped in a strong grasp, and at the same time being trapped by an argument she had left herself open for. She had told him she was afraid of public opinion, and now they were far removed from the public eye.

His voice came like the murmur of a low surf. "You've made a study of holding people away from you, haven't you? You've bottled up every bit of human emotion you have and stored it away where no one can find it. You're afraid of new experiences, and new people that come along. Don't be afraid of life, Christine! Let me kiss you, let me free you. Stop shivering and stop being afraid."

"I am not afraid of life!" she said, bravely thrusting her chin up into the air.

"Then prove it," Nick said thickly.

This time it was Christine who reached out for Nick, thrusting her body up against his, stretching her arms out as if grasping for the gold ring on the merry-go-round as she reached up around his neck, pulling his face down toward hers. And then when he kissed her it was a mutual experience, both sharing in the process of giving pleasure and taking it.

Christine felt like a surfer who had waited too long for the ninth wave. And now she was finally on that perfect ride that seemed to go on forever on its way to the beach. She felt suspended in time, as if the empty blue sea curled endlessly beneath her, lifting her higher and higher on that thrilling ride. Shore seemed very far away. She was, at last, enjoying life, nursing from it every last moment of fulfillment. And Nick seemed intent on making her daring glide along the top of the sea as memorable as he could, using his lips against hers, and then against her cheeks and neck, to bring her to life with a shuddering gasp for air, as if she'd come up from a long underwater swim.

"You are a passionate, desirable woman. Will you believe me when I tell you that?" he was saying, close to her ear. Then he let a trail of soft and tantalizing kisses lead him down her neck from behind her ear to the modestly protective high collar of her gown. Then his head swung lazily to the other side, and he began the same seductive pattern, this time interspersed with comments she could barely hear.

"I want you, Christine. I want to see you fly and soar, become the exciting woman you can be. I must have you."

"Oh, Nick. I don't know if I can take this. I'm just not ready for this." She stepped back away from him, further into the darkness.

"You seem more than ready to me, my sweet."

She thought about her words carefully before she spoke again. "I've been without male companionship, affection if you will, for a long time. It's overpowering me. I think I'm too vulnerable, too lonely, to know what I'm getting into. To think about it rationally."

She turned her face up toward the star-sprinkled sky, and felt with relief the soothing caress of the heavy tropical air against her burning cheeks.

"Since when does rational thinking have anything to do with it? We're talking about feelings, here."

"Please take me home."

"If that's what you want."

"Yes, right now."

Their drive home was wordless, and Nick followed her into the house tiptoeing as she was too, so as not to disturb Mrs. Hanover or the servants. He followed her upstairs, since his room was near hers, but stopped with her outside her door.

She leaned back and stared up into his face. His eyes seemed like those in the portraits the local artists loved to paint on black velvet. They were soft and gently appealing.

He reached out and took her by the shoulders, then ran his hands sensuously down her body, rolling them over her curves as he closed his eyes as if imagining what couldn't be seen beneath the yards of fabric concealing her.

"Now that I know what goodies you're hiding under these ceremonial robes you hide yourself in, I can't wait to get you out of them."

"Maybe we can go to the beach together tomorrow," she suggested demurely, and started to turn around and open the door.

"Beach tomorrow, hell! Forget tomorrow. Today isn't over with yet. I'm coming in right now with you." And before she knew it he had pushed her inside her room and closed the door behind both of them.

"Nick, I thought you understood. I told you, I'm too vulnerable for this kind of relationship with anyone."

"I heard what you said, and I sympathize. But trust me, trust your feelings. I won't hurt you. Let yourself go. Take a chance, before it's too late, will you?"

She crossed the room to the wide windowseat beneath the view out to the Hanover gardens. The air, sweet-scented after its passage over a multitude of blooming plants, wafted into the room, creating a romantic aura that nightly mocked Christine's solitude.

"Please leave my room right away," she said, sitting down. She was desperately afraid that if he touched her now her will power would dissolve.

His tone was louder when he answered her, because he was clear across the room. "I guess I read you all wrong. I thought you were opening up to me. What's gone wrong?"

"Sh!" she said with a start. "Mrs. Hanover's room is right down the hall. She'll hear you."

"Must every conversation in this house be held in whispers?" he said in a raspy tone that was just as loud.

He was standing with his tuxedo jacket flung open, his hands in his pockets. His vexation was obvious.

"You must disregard what happened in that romantic garden. I forgot myself for a moment, but it is all over," she told him, looking away from his tempting, attracting male physique.

"You didn't forget yourself, you found yourself." He crossed the room slowly, as if approaching an untamed animal. Then he sat down on the cushion beside her and reached up to touch the gardenia in her hair. "Your flower is still fresh and alive. And so are you. You can't deny it forever."

He pulled the flower from her hair and held it out to her to show her, then he reached back up to her intricate formal hairdo again and began pulling out pins and stretching the tightly coiled strands loose about her neck as she trembled slightly.

"Why do you wear your hair in such tight control? Why

don't you let it flow loose and free onto your shoulders, as it should?"

"I like to wear it up, out of the way."

"And you must wear it the way Mrs. Hanover's hairdresser fixes it, and dress the way Mrs. Hanover's dressmaker decides you must, and act the way Mrs. Hanover says you should, and talk in whispers for fear Mrs. Hanover will be disturbed."

"That's not it," she protested weakly.

"You are so busy conforming to what that woman expects of you that you can't think for yourself any more. You'd do anything to please her, wouldn't you? That's the stiff price you're paying, don't you see? Because you want, above all else, to go on living here in the plush, safe surroundings of the Hanover mansion where you can escape any of the real world lurking about outside."

"No, you're wrong. I could leave here at any time. In fact, I've been thinking about getting a place of my own and moving away from Diamond Head."

Nick stood up and began pacing the floor, his aggravation tensing the long muscles of his thighs and forearms so that he marched stiffly. "I don't believe you! You're stuck here as surely as if you were under a lifetime sentence to prison. A very pleasant prison, I grant you that," he said, sweeping a straight arm around her beautifully furnished suite, "but a prison nonetheless."

Christine saw her opportunity to lead him to the door, and hopefully, out of her room. She wanted his disturbing presence outside her door as soon as possible.

"You'll no doubt go on living here forever, safe and cloistered, protected by the Hanover property and the Hanover name. Then when your role as the widow of a hero becomes dim and boring, you will marry Andrew Hanover and life will go right on, predestined."

At Christine's shocked look he quickly responded, "Yes, I'm sure Mrs. Hanover has Andrew all picked out for you. Can't you see that? She knows, even if you don't, that someday you'll become a bit restless and dissatisfied. A good planned marriage is the customary cure for that condition. And the only man in the world worthy of David's widow is obviously another Hanover, in her eyes. And you'll probably go meekly along with the plan, like a good little girl."

Christine stood facing him, shock and anger lighting up her eyes. "You must be a truly imaginative writer, to make up fantasies like that," she hissed at him. "I think you are despicable, with your stupid accusations." She opened the door, and spoke the rest of her tirade in a hoarse whisper. "Get out and leave me alone."

She wanted to slam the door, but didn't dare make such a scene. She closed it quietly after he'd gone out. Then she went over and picked up the gardenia from the floor near the windowseat where it had fallen. She tucked it between the pages of the poetry book on her bedside table to preserve it, and went to her dressing room to get ready for bed, mumbling to herself, "Me? Marry Andrew? Ridiculous!"

CHAPTER FOUR

THE NEXT MORNING it was well after nine when Christine woke up, and realizing she'd slept too late to accompany her mother-in-law to church, she dawdled over her shower and killed time tidying up her room before finally going downstairs. She dreaded the prospect of encountering Nick at the breakfast table or being alone in the house with him.

She knew that last night she had revealed her clearly mixed emotions concerning him. Now as she played and replayed the scene in the hotel garden when she had shamelessly thrown herself in his arms and wantonly enjoyed the moments that followed, she berated herself for letting Nick see that he had a power over her she couldn't resist.

He was the snake in Eden, he was temptation itself, tantalizing her with visions of a carefree and irresponsible life of pleasure-seeking. And she knew her destiny was quite different. It was to serve David's memory, to devote herself to perpetuating the brave story of his deeds. And she didn't intend to deviate from that straight path, no matter how compelling the attraction.

"Mr. Carruthers leave note he be gone all day."

Mrs. Wang's voice came as a shock to her, for she hadn't even seen the woman in the dark dining room. Christine went to the long plantation shutters that were kept closed over the windows and threw them open, letting the sparkling Polynesian sunlight stream into the room.

"So I put breakfast all away. But now you're here, I fix."

"Just some coffee for now. Mrs. Hanover will be home for brunch soon and I'll join her," Christine said.

Thank goodness she would be free to talk with her mother-in-law alone and uninterrupted today, she thought as she stirred her coffee. She could describe her suspicions concerning Mr. Nicolas Carruthers, the internationally famous journalist who was here to make sport of their life stories on the pages of his best-selling exposé. She could help Florence Hanover plan a way to be rid of him. The serpent would be expelled from the garden.

Above her head the large wooden blades of the big ceiling fan made a droning noise as they spun round and round, moving the air in lazy drafts about the warm room. Christine leaned her elbow on the table and rested her cheek on her open palm. She felt empty and sad, overcome with feelings of loneliness that she seldom had time to think about. They were always lurking just outside the carefully organized structure of her busy days, but she rarely had meditative moments alone when they could catch up with her and overtake her.

"Andrew, close up those shutters, will you?" Mrs. Hanover's crisp instructions woke her from her melancholia with a start. "Christine, have you lost your mind sitting here in the glaring sun?"

"I didn't hear you come in. Good morning, Andrew, Mrs. Hanover."

"Andrew will join us for brunch today. When I met him at church he said he had some project in mind to do with you today," Mrs. Hanover said, letting Andrew pull out a chair for her at the head of the long table. "You were missed this morning, Christine. Don't let this sleeping in on Sunday become a habit."

As the serving girl brought in pitchers of juice and platters of scrambled eggs and cinnamon rolls, Christine regrouped her plans. Perhaps it was better to tell them both at once of her feelings about Nick. After all, Andrew was the one who had warned her to keep Nick on the right track, so he already had his doubts about the man.

"Andrew asked you how the fleet party was," Florence Hanover said, repeating a question to Christine with obvious annoyance.

"Oh, fine. I danced with Admiral Elliott and he sends his best to you."

"Isn't that nice," she said, truly pleased to be remembered by one of such high rank.

Christine's thoughts faded away from the breakfast table, back to the dance. She began to remember Admiral Elliott's strangely aloof attitude toward Nick and his book project, almost as if he wanted to avoid all connection with it. And what had he called Christine's life: empty hero worship? What had he meant by that?

"Oh, yes. Mr. Carruthers seemed to enjoy the party." She answered one of Andrew's meaningless questions almost as if she'd been listening to him. "And speaking of Mr. Carruthers..."

"Yes?"

"Yes?"

Andrew and his mother both put down their forks to stare at Christine with rapt attention. But at the mention of Nick's name Christine suddenly pictured him being led onto the dance floor with Linda Elliott. She realized she never would have remembered Linda's affair with David if Nick Carruthers hadn't come to town, flogging her dead memory to life with his infernal questions and his disrespect for people's fond but inaccurate memories of the past.

"Christine, do keep your mind on what you're saying," Mrs. Hanover said sharply.

Andrew had finished eating and pushed his chair back from the table to light up a cigarette. "I believe you were speaking of Mr. Carruthers' work, and that's just what I came to see you about this morning."

Christine stared at him, wondering if he had guessed what was on her mind. Maybe he had decided, all on his own, to cut this project off right now and send Nick back to New York. That would mean no more revelations about the past, no more remembered sorrows, no more harsh reality to face. They could go back to living their unquestioning lives.

"I want you to help me dig out some of David's things from the storage shed," Andrew was saying. "As soon as you're through eating we should get at it."

Suddenly Christine knew that she was not going to tell Andrew and his mother what she suspected. Not just yet. Some odd compulsion to find out what more Nick might unearth had stopped her. Here was an opportunity to put her life back on a footing in the real world, to separate the dream from the reality, to know once and for all if she was living a lie. She couldn't resist the opportunity to find out.

Somehow, remembering her late husband's unfaithfulness, his desperate search for ego fulfillment, her own diligent attempts to be fair to him, to give him plenty of room to grow and change, had lifted one heavy rock of guilt out of the pack she was carrying on her back. The truth did not hurt; the truth did not need to be destructive. If it tore down false demi-gods, it replaced them with more honest values. She blinked her eyes to try to pull herself back into the prattling conservation flying back and forth past her unhearing ears.

"I agree with Andrew. The more we can tell Mr. Carruthers about our dear boy, right back to his happy childhood and his brilliant prep school days, the better the book will be," David's mother was saying, her face alight with happy dreams of the past.

Taking a typically nervous puff of his cigarette, Andrew said, "Our Mr. Carruthers will be glad to study whatever we can dig out of the storeroom, I'm sure. He seems a hardworking enough writer, don't you think, Christine? I mean, in spite of his somewhat whimsical sense of humor. That's just typical of the creative character, I suppose."

"Yes, he's very industrious," Christine said quietly. She rubbed her hands together in her lap. Now she'd given Nicolas Carruthers her endorsement! She had let the opportunity pass to expose him as a traitor. She had not told them that Nick's presence here at this temple to David's memory was irreverent: that he would not worship the idol with the same blind devotion the Hanover clan agreed to. She had not warned them that this man came seeking truth, and that he didn't care what comfortable myths the search destroyed.

She wondered what had motivated her silence. Had she offered Nick this protection because she wanted to pursue the search with him, or simply because his expert kisses had muddled her senses? Was it a love of truth, or the need to draw closer to the warm and accepting embrace of his attentions?

As soon as breakfast was over, Andrew led her out the side door of the house, past the garages to the big old garden shack utilized as a general storeroom. The room was full of a lifetime of memorabilia, for the Hanover family discarded nothing. Cartons and unusable furniture had been collected here since the family moved into this house shortly after World War II. That was when Florence Hanover came to the islands to join her husband, who was assigned to administer the postwar recovery of Pearl Harbor, and they had purchased this Diamond Head showplace so she could entertain and otherwise advance her husband's career.

"What we must find is that box of David's sports awards. And all his papers from Punahou School."

"Do you really think any of that has any importance?" Christine dared to venture.

Andrew stopped moving cardboard boxes around and looked at her incredulously. "Everything about David is important. I'm sure you know that better than anyone. You saw a side to him none of the rest of us could ever know . . . the personal things, I mean, that only a wife could share."

His own words had embarrassed him, and he quickly stuck another cigarette in his mouth and lit it, expelling some dismissing words with the smoke. "I'm sorry. I didn't mean to intrude into your private memories."

Andrew was so prudish that Christine wondered how he had ever managed, even in his young college days, to attract a wife and get her to move all the way out here from her

New England home. That young bride, Emily, had contracted "rock fever" within a few years and left Andrew, and the island, never to return. It was said that the confinement here on a small island isolated in the middle of vast ocean expanse had driven her to this unthinkable desertion. The family had rarely spoken of her since the divorce, until earlier this year when Jenny, the product of that brief marriage, had appeared on the scene.

"It's all right, Andrew. Those memories do fade somewhat with time, become less painful," she said reassuringly.

"I hope the memories never fade, but that your sadness will, Christine. So that you can begin life afresh. So that you can find happiness again."

He moved closer to her, and Christine studied him with widened eyes. He seemed to be trying to work up the nerve to come closer to her, emotionally as well as physically. He put one hand on her shoulder.

"I even dare to hope that someday I might be able to bring that happiness back for you."

Oh, no. What is he trying to say? she thought with panic.

"You mustn't feel responsible for me," she said, a look of fetching confusion upon her face that she didn't intend.

"Oh, but I want to be, don't you see?" Andrew said, dropping his cigarette to the floor and stamping it out quickly as he lunged forward to grasp her in an awkward embrace.

Christine knew she had to handle the situation diplomatically, so she forced herself not to jump from his grasp with the revulsion she felt. She rested her face against his shoulder as he held her close to him. He seemed as bewildered as to where to go from here as Christine was. So she began to speak softly.

"It is too soon to talk about it, Andrew. As much as I admire you, I'm just not ready to make any changes in my life."

"Of course. Forgive me. I promise I'll give you all the time you need, my dear. Just know that I'm here and waiting when you feel ready to accept my comfort."

He'll wait for years, if necessary. He'll always be here, as inevitable as my shadow. The thought depressed her.

One moment of weakness, one mood of loneliness too massive to bear, and she would find herself with a quick and
ready solution—a new Hanover husband, and Mrs. Hanover's continued blessings.

She forced him to return to the project at hand, and soon
he was so busy reorganizing the storeroom that he'd forgotten his descent into a moment of wild emotion.

As they moved scrapbooks and boxes of trophies outside
and stacked them on the grass, Christine suddenly had an
annoying thought.

"Oh, damn!" she blurted out, and then tried to excuse
her outburst by pretending she'd dropped a box on her foot.

"Naughty girl, watch your language," Andrew warned
her as if he were talking to his daughter.

But Christine ignored him, for she was fuming over how
accurately Nick had been able to see something coming
toward her that she had missed. How angry she had been
when he predicted this insane plan the Hanovers had for her
future.

Never ones to leave anything to chance, to the erratic
flopping about of fate, Mrs. Hanover and Andrew probably
subconsciously pictured the precise timetable for Christine's
future, year by year into perpetuity. And Nick had figured
out their intentions, while she had never even noticed the
clues.

"I feel terribly tired, Andrew. That party last night has
left me worn out. I think I'll go upstairs and rest if you
don't mind."

"Go right along, dear. I'm going to take a few of these
things inside and go over them with Mother. We'll sort
them out before we pass them on to Carruthers. We wouldn't
want any detention-hall notices or misconduct warnings to
slip into the official record, now would we? David could
be a bit of a scamp when he wanted to, I remember."

Christine stayed in her room all afternoon, trying to sleep
but again and again disturbed by the vexing realization that
Nick Carruthers had been able so easily to discern the pattern
of her life, even to foreseeing this startling revelation from
Andrew. He had been right about this. He had seen what

she had closed her eyes to. Maybe he was right about other things. He told her she also closed her eyes to life itself, that she kept herself rigidly scheduled and programmed with things she didn't really want to do just so she wouldn't have time to think and to feel. Was he right about that?

She heard the sound of a car driving up in front of the house and went to her window. One brief curve of the driveway was visible from the side portion of her bay window. She leaned around to see a taxi just pulling away, so she assumed that Nick had returned from whatever errand he had spent the day on. Then she sat down and dreamily gazed into the garden until her glance was drawn back toward the driveway and garage area.

Something in the air made her muscles tense, her ears strain for sounds of danger. She took a deep breath and realized it was the faint smell of smoke in the air that had alarmed her. Now squinting carefully toward the direction of the storage shed she thought she could just barely discern a thin whisp of smoke against the bright yellow canopy of blossoms created by the Golden Shower trees that lined the driveway.

She jumped up and ran out the door. The first person she saw was Mrs. Wang carrying laundry down the hall. The old Chinese woman looked alarmed, never having seen Christine move so fast.

"The storage shed is on fire. Call the fire department," she cried out over her shoulder.

As soon as she reached the shed she was relieved to see that there was only a great deal of smoke seeping out through the old wooden roof, no flames in sight. She threw open the big double doors and rushed inside, intent on saving what she could of the family heirlooms and mementos before they were damaged. She headed at once for the boxes she and Andrew had been examining piled in one corner. One was marked "David's Uniforms," and she grabbed it up with both hands just as she heard a sickening swoosh of air behind her.

The fire had apparently smoldered inside the airless room for several hours, ever since Andrew Hanover had so hastily discarded his cigarette on the floor. But when Christine opened the doors, a gush of air came inside with her, and now the fresh oxygen was giving the fire the draft of energy it required. Flames burst up all around her, and she knew she had to get out of the shed at once.

A burning cinder fell on the cardboard box she was carrying and she snuffed at it with shaking hands, momentarily forgetting her need to escape. She clutched the box under one arm, and with the other patted out the tiny bursts of flame that were licking at the sleeves of her blouse and the hem of her skirt.

She twirled first one way and then another. She had lost her sense of direction, her eyes were so shrouded by the curtains of smoke. She stumbled against an old chest of drawers, then turned and found herself up against a wall. There seemed no way out of the inferno that was fueling itself into greater destructiveness all around her.

She began to cough, her chest heaving with painful attempts to bring air into her lungs, and when no fresh air came, her mind exploded with panic. She threw herself down on the floor and began crawling, desperate to find more air close to the ground, hoping that the next direction she would try would bring her to the door.

This room couldn't be over twenty feet square. I can't be lost, I'm only disoriented. I mustn't panic. I've tried that way, here's a table leg, that's the right way. The door must be just ahead. Ahead. My head! Oooo . . .

She reached up and grasped a burning piece of wood from where it had landed painfully in her hair, and threw it away. Then she thrust her head under the box she was pushing along in front of her, hoping it would protect her.

I'll rest a minute and get my bearings. My hands! Oh, my hands are tingling. If only I could use them to push myself forward. It can't be much farther. But they hurt. They . . .

"Chris! Where are you?"

She lifted her head, knocking the box aside.

"My God! I almost stepped on you, hidden there on the

floor. Come on, let's get you out of here. The ceiling's
going to fall any minute."

With a groan of urgency, Nick stooped down and lifted
her into his arms as easily as if she were a child, then
stumbled with her through the burning debris and out of the
shed.

"Oh, Nick," she sobbed, then her head fell back against
his supportive arm, her eyes closed as she concentrated on
drawing the cool sweet air into her body.

Reacting to her sudden limpness, Nick dropped her
abruptly on the grass and began shaking her by the shoulders
and calling her name. The wail of sirens on the fire engines
heading toward them down Diamond Head Road became
louder and she opened her eyes.

"The box. Where's the box I was carrying?" she asked.

But as soon as she'd opened her eyes Nick stilled her
words with a quick kiss. "Thank God you're alive. I saw
you run in there, but I was afraid I couldn't find you in
time, with all that smoke."

Christine saw an expression on his face that she'd never
seen before on anyone else's. He knelt beside her, watching
her with total absorption, as if her very act of breathing
were a miracle. His eyes were trained unwaveringly on her
face, and he never looked away, even when a fire engine
pulled up to park a few feet away from his legs. His eyes
were overly bright, sparkling with the tears that the smoke
had caused, and red-rimmed where he had probably rubbed
at them.

"The fire, it was all around me and I couldn't see to find
my way out." She wanted to tell him just how terrifying it
had been, but he was so concerned with her well-being that
his caring was transformed into anger.

"Why did you ever do such a stupid thing? Why did you
go in there?"

"I wanted to bring out as much as I could. Where is that
box?"

Christine knew she wasn't thinking clearly. The carton
of old uniforms wasn't important. But she was obsessed
with finding it because she didn't want to think any more

about all the horror of those last few moments in the store-room: the flames, the burning cinders, the smoke.

"Here come the paramedics to check you over, so I'll go ask the firemen about that blessed box of yours. I'm sure it's right inside the door."

Andrew and his mother came out of the house then, and when Mrs. Hanover saw Christine, her dress scorched, her body stained with soot, she let out a sharp cry of shock and ran back inside to call the family doctor. Andrew rushed over to the shed and began calling instructions to the firemen as to which valuables to try to pull out of the burning building.

A few moments later, as one paramedic removed a blood pressure cuff from her arm and gave a satisfied nod to the other, Nick approached Christine, the battered box in his hands with the lettering still visible on the side.

"So you almost gave your life just to try to save some old military trappings? You're hopeless!" He threw the box on the ground beside her. "Your devotion to the past is so stubborn, and so blind, that you almost got yourself killed, and for what? You little fool."

During the next few days Christine was confined to her bed, on doctor's orders. Both of her hands were bandaged so that she felt completely helpless, and very frustrated by the inactivity. She was allowed visitors, and Nick stopped by almost every afternoon for a quick, impersonal visit. To Christine's surprise, he was accompanied by Jenny on the second day, and then again on the third and fourth days. They gave no explanations, just came into the room together, stayed for a few moments of polite inquiries about the improvement of the burns on her hands, and then left together.

As soon as the door had closed behind them on that last visit, Christine jumped up out of bed and threw her robe about herself. She was not going to stay off her feet any longer, and to demonstrate that fact to the world she began making up her bed, her hands clumsy in their gauze wrappings, but not in the least painful. When she was about halfway through the project there was a knock at her door, and she went to find Nick there.

"Aha! When you're all alone and no one can see you, you dress like a showgirl. I've now discovered your secret vice, haven't I?"

She was wearing a silk kimono she'd found in China-town, with a pattern in the colors of the Ming period pottery, rich cobalt blue against a pure white background, with soft peach flowers.

"Did you know that the strippers in Las Vegas wear kimonos like that between their shows?" he said walking into her room. "Just to keep the breezes off."

She held up her hands in front of her. "And do they keep the breezes off their hands this way?" she mocked.

"All right. Quit trying to make a play for my sympathy. I know you were wounded in action. I've put in your name for a Purple Heart. When can those bandages come off?" he asked.

"As a matter of fact, the doctor said I could take them off today." With a brave toss of her head she turned toward her bedside table and pulled off the strips of bandage. She was relieved to find her hands a bit red and sunburned looking, but otherwise undamaged.

"See! Everything works. Now I can play the piano." She wriggled all ten fingers up in the air toward Nick.

"If only you knew how to play the piano," he laughed, unfooled.

Nick's mood was playful, but there seemed something serious lurking in the shadowy places around his eyes.

"Why did you come back? Did you forget to tell me something?"

"Yes, I forgot to tell you that I love your hair that way."

She reached up suddenly and gathered her long tresses into a bunch at the back of her neck with one hand.

"I couldn't use my hands to fix it before, and besides, it won't stay in a French twist when I'm in bed," she said, flustered to have been caught with her hair, and her self-protection, down.

"I've often wondered how you wear your hair in bed,"

he said, giving her a humorously lecherous look. "I've pictured you rolling wildly about on the pillowcase, that French twist coming all undone." He must have seen the protest springing to her lips, because he stopped her with a quick question. "How do you do that twist thing, anyway?"

"Well, you pull all your hair to one side, and pin it like this, then . . . Oh, you don't really want to hear all this." She laughed, finishing up the project before her dresser mirror as he strolled over to her windowseat and made himself comfortable watching her.

She was amazed at herself. Only a few weeks ago she would have been totally unnerved at the idea of having a man in her room while she was barely dressed. Especially a man who liked to rile her with his provocative talk. Perhaps she was changing, becoming more relaxed in her attitudes. But Mrs. Hanover hadn't changed any, she knew that.

"Perhaps you'd better tell me what you came back to say and be on your way before Mrs. Hanover comes looking for you," she said.

"Oh, I've got the perfect cover story. I can stay as long as I want. Even your strict chaperones can't object to my visiting the wounded. That's a noble cause. Does it make you uncomfortable, having me here?"

She lowered her eyes and said quietly, "Yes, it does."

"I've tried to leave you alone the last few days. I really had hoped that you'd use this convalescent time for some thinking. I want you to come to your own conclusions, make peace with the past all by yourself."

She leaned back against the dresser, her head down, unable to look into those eyes of his that were capable of reading her thoughts so clearly.

"Is that what you came to tell me?"

"I came to apologize for acting the beast the last time we were alone together here in this room. When we came home from the dance. Do you remember?"

She sat down on the edge of her bed. "Yes, I remember."

"I was prying into your life, making you uncomfortable, forcing myself on you when you weren't ready. I know that now. But honestly, Christine, sometimes you drive me quite insane."

He ruffled his waves of dark hair with his fingers, then absently pushed them back down into place again. "You're so damned luscious and young and appealing. You have a lusty sense of humor and a lusty...well...anyway. Whatever you have, you hide it under that phony old maid routine. But I can see through it, and I want to break you free of it."

Christine felt her eyes fill with tears of frustration. He was right, and she knew it. But she'd never admitted it before. She felt a wild urge to go over and throw herself into his arms again. She wanted to thank him, and tell him not to give up on her just yet. She was changing.

"Dammit. I didn't come here to berate you. And here I'm going at it again. I came to tell you that I won't bother you with my physical attentions any more. I was wrong to try to force something on you before you were ready. And you were right; the only way we can work together is if I keep my distance."

She looked at him with surprise. "And it's terribly important to you that we work together, isn't it? I mean, you need my help with that book, don't you? And you're afraid that something might happen, that I might refuse to help you."

She hated herself for all the ugly suspicions that kept creeping into their relationship. But Nick seemed oblivious to the implications of her words.

"Jenny offered to fill in for you while you've been laid up. The past few days she's actually taken time away from her beach buddies to drive me around to my appointments. She's gotten quite involved and interested."

"Oh. I see," Christine said, a cold feeling rushing up within her. Nick had apparently switched his attack to the youngest Hanover woman, figuring he could use her the same way he had planned to use Christine. And Jenny was young and impressionable, and would be quite thrilled to give the famous author any help she could. She'd merely

transferred her search for thrills from the surf to more sophisticated sports.

"She even called up Admiral Elliott and got us an appointment yesterday afternoon at his home."

"Admiral Elliott talked to you?"

"Well, he never showed up, but I had a nice long interview with his daughter."

Christine's chill turned to a freezing splash as she remembered just what Linda Elliott could tell him. Surely she
would not have told Nick about her affair with David. One
thing the girl had learned from being an Admiral's daughter
was to be discreet! Christine's thoughts raced ahead madly.
Linda might hint around in her flirty, bragging way, but she
would be smart enough not to give the writer any real quot-
able facts.

But even if Nick only guessed the truth, it would give
him a clearer picture of the real David Hanover—human
and fallible. And quite different from the official family
portrait of him.

Nick was still talking, listing the military men and family
friends he had talked to in the last few days. Several of
them were people Christine would have kept him away from:
an Ensign who had driven David home drunk several nights,
a jealous friend who always chided David for making rapid
advancement in the Navy only because his father had been
an Admiral. Christine hadn't thought about these people in
years, and now with Jenny's help Nick had somehow found
them, and pried open their buried secrets. No sense of propriety or family allegiance would hold Jenny back. There
was something wild and rebellious about the girl that would
probably make her enjoy setting off a family scandal, creating some excitement she would be at the center of.

Christine stood up so suddenly that her head began to
spin with dizziness. She felt as if Nick were presenting her
with a Pandora's Box, bursting at the seams and spilling
out its contents of human frailties.

Nick must have noticed her drawn facial expression,
because he jumped up and came to her side. "Here, let me
help you back into bed. You look very pale; I don't think

you should be doing so much quite yet. Has something upset you?"

She knew he was studying her reactions like a trained cross-examiner, looking for a telltale sign, a guilty flinch, that would confirm whatever evil suspicions he was forming.

"I've read all your books now, you know," she said, pulling out of his grasp. "I know just what kind of a writer you are. And I'm afraid you are not the proper person to be working on this project."

"And just what kind of a writer am I?" he asked her, his lips narrowing ominously.

"You're a good old-fashioned muckraker, and you sensationalize every story you touch. I know that's why you're doing such thorough research, going to such great lengths to interview every person who ever knew David. You're hoping to find out something awful about him. Well, you won't! He was a good and honorable man," she hurled at him in desperation.

"He was no saint, and you know that if you'll just admit it. You're sacrificing your youth, and if you don't wake up pretty soon you'll probably sacrifice the rest of your life to a false god, to a figment of your romantic imagination. Do you know what Shakespeare said? 'Tis mad idolatry to make the service greater than the god.' And that's just what you've done. He isn't worth it. He wasn't worthy of you when you married him and he isn't worthy of your guilt and sorrow now."

"You don't care if you slander the reputation of a good man, just so it sells your book. You're going to drag this whole family down into the mud with your scandalmongering, just to satisfy your thirst for success, just to feed the rumor mills and satisfy the sensation-hungry readers you write for."

"He isn't worth it, Christine. You're devoting yourself to a lie," Nick said, his temper having receded like a tide, leaving him sad and wasted-looking, his voice so low she could barely hear it.

"How can you say that?" she asked, sitting up straighter in bed.

"The man you've devoted yourself to was not the great man you've tried to make him into. And he wasn't a hero, either."

Nick paused as if he were almost afraid to go on. But he must have judged her strong enough to take what he had to tell her. In spite of the angry words they had just exchanged, he came to the bed, sat down on the edge beside her, and took one of her slender arms into his hand almost tenderly, gazing down at the reddened hand with a distracted look, the pupils of his eyes dark, dilated as if he were looking beyond her hand to something larger and more significant that it represented.

He continued slowly, cautiously, breaking each new fact over her head like relentless waves.

"That dangerous mission of David's in the China Sea. It was actually a routine patrol. And his so-called 'hostile encounter' was with a native fishing boat that had wandered off course a bit. His rash action of firing on them illegally could have led to an international incident. As it was, it led to his being wounded, probably by the guns of his own ship in the chaos that followed. If he hadn't died of those wounds he would have been brought up for court martial."

"You are lying." She took her hand from his grasp.

"You said yourself that my research is thorough," he said slowly, getting up off the bed and walking to the door. He was shaking his head, as if the true story was as depressing to him as it was shocking to her.

He let himself out with hardly a sound after saying, "You weren't married to any hero."

CHAPTER FIVE

THE TEMPERATURE WAS in the mid-eighties, but while that usually meant pleasant conditions, today a Kona wind came across the island from the leeward direction, and without the usual brisk tradewinds to keep the air fresh the weather was humid. Christine mopped at her brow with a handkerchief as she got out of her car, uncomfortable in the damp heat that was so rare in the Hawaiian Islands.

Today she had a difficult mission ahead of her, and she'd come home armed for it with a bundle of flowers under her arm. As she entered the house she unwrapped them. When Mrs. Wang came to greet her, she asked her for a vase and went to work immediately arranging the bright red anthuriums and the exotic orange bird-of-paradise blooms for the entry hall table.

"Mrs. Wang tells me you've brought flowers, Christine. How very sweet of you. Oh!"

Mrs. Hanover came down the hall from the living room and stopped short at the sight of the long-stemmed flowers of such shocking hues that they looked like a fireworks display going off in the dim foyer.

"Next time, Christine, just bring greenery. Those gaudy things make our home look like some Waikiki tourist trap."

She turned on her heel to march solemnly back to the living room, and Christine followed behind her, giving a playful salute to each portrait in the gallery they were passing, knowing that Mrs. Hanover wasn't quick enough to turn around and catch her at it.

When they were seated in the stiff loveseats opposite each other on the Aubusson carpet in the center of the room, like opposing teams squaring off before a game, Mrs. Hanover asked her, "Where have you been all day? You left me no word of your whereabouts."

Knowing that now was as good a time as any, Christine took a deep breath and shot back at her, "I've been out apartment hunting."

Her mother-in-law looked stunned. "Why would you be looking at apartments?" she asked, giving the final word a disdainful sniff.

"For myself. A place for me to move into."

"But why? You are a Hanover, and the family home is right here."

"This is your home, Mrs. Hanover. I've never had a place of my own, and I think it's time."

"That's a ridiculous notion. Your place is here with me. I want you to drop this nonsense at once."

"It's too late. I've already leased a place."

"Hooray, hooray!" came the booming voice from the doorway, and Nick strode into the room with his hands clasped above his head in a victory sign. "So you're finally going to show the world you're all grown up."

Then, taking notice of the cold silence coming from Mrs. Hanover as she went to her wing chair in the corner, he decided to use his talent to weave spells with words.

"This is long overdue. Christine's period of mourning was attracting unfavorable attention. I heard it mentioned at the dance just the other night—by Admiral Elliott, I believe. It is unnatural for grief to be carried on so long. This move proves she is ready to face life again on its own terms, not hiding away somewhere like a coward, unworthy of the Hanover name."

With a wry smile, Christine tapped her fingers on the tight upholstery beside her, in time to the snare drums and military trumpets she thought she could hear faintly accompanying his overblown speech. But Mrs. Hanover was falling for it. She was too proud a woman not to. Some lingering doubts, however, remained.

"But Christine, our schedules are planned so that we go places together," she pouted, selfishly considering the fact that she might be losing her private chauffeur.

"We'll still have those wonderful Wednesday lunches at the Cannon Club, Mother," Christine said. She failed to mention any of the many other appointments they shared. "I plan to spend more time at NASAP. Kim needs my help there, and we have a whole new class starting up next week. The drive from here to Pearl Harbor takes me over forty minutes."

"Where did you find an apartment?" Nick asked her.

"It's in the Aiea area near Pearl City. And it's ready immediately."

Nick stood up at strict attention. "Then I await assignment, ma'am. I stand ready to carry boxes and move suitcases. Get upstairs there and start packing. Mrs. Hanover and I are going to toast your launching with a drink while you get to work. Gin and tonic, as usual, Mrs. H?"

Christine knew his plan was to keep Mrs. Hanover so occupied that no more unpleasant notice would be taken of her leaving, and for that she was grateful. Somehow he managed to keep up his cheerleading performance all through dinner, telling stories about his travels through the Orient, and giving Mrs. Hanover no time to think up impediments to Christine's ambitious new plans for independence.

As soon as the last bite of coconut cake had been consumed, Nick pushed his chair back and announced, "I hope you have your things ready to be loaded in the car."

"There isn't really very much to take." Christine had accumulated very little of her own during her years of marriage and widowhood, and all her possessions fit nicely inside one set of luggage and four or five boxes.

Mrs. Hanover looked startled by how fast events were moving. "I think I'd better call Andrew. He manages your financial accounts, Christine. He should advise you before you do something so rash."

Nick could see objections and complaints coming, so he hustled everyone out of the dining room at once. Before Mrs. Hanover could summon Andrew or think up any persuasive arguments with which to dampen Christine's resolved spirit, Nick had the car loaded and they were driving away like conspirators on an elopement. He had accomplished the move with almost the same frantic dispatch as Christine's apartment-hunting.

But once they were inside the car, driving through the cloying damp air of the moonless night, Christine felt sympathy for the old woman she'd left behind.

"She'll be all alone in that big house. She has very few friends. She's counted on me for every bit of activity she has in her life."

"That's not your fault. She made that choice, to devote the rest of her life to paying homage to her late husband and son, making a mausoleum of her home. That's her sacrifice, if she wants to make it. You've just made another choice, and I'm proud of you for doing it. I'm sure it wasn't easy."

"I feel the way I did right after my father died. You know, my mother went all to pieces. She started drinking; she couldn't cope with it. And I had to be so strong, so decisive for her, when inside I was just as full of lost and lonely feelings as she was. That's how I feel now. Brave on the outside and scared to death on the inside."

Christine had gone from her father to her mother to David and then to Mrs. Hanover in her search for security. And now for the first time she was utterly alone. She remembered that every time she'd tried to find her confidence in someone else she had been disappointed. Now that she had only her own resources to draw on, perhaps she'd at last found what she was looking for—her own strong capability for independence to depend on.

"Just speaking out loud to me about your fears took real bravery. You're opening up, revealing things, exposing yourself for the first time," Nick was saying.

"It feels good to speak honestly. Also, it feels kind of nice to be responsible to no one for once. Why, I can get up at three in the morning and make myself a peanut butter sandwich if I want. I probably won't do that, but it's just knowing that I can, without disturbing anyone."

"You're free," he said, and he reached over to pat her knee in the dark. "I want you to learn to appreciate that. I want you to learn that being alone does not mean being lonely. I hope you'll learn to love living on your own. I'm going to leave you plenty of time to adjust to it."

"What do you mean?"

"I'm going to give you room, stay out of your way."

Christine wished he wouldn't bother to make up such an elaborate excuse, just because he had now transferred his attentions to Jenny. Why didn't he just come out and tell her that he no longer needed her help on the project? She began to speculate on where he might have been all day. If he'd been out with Jenny doing more interviews, she worried about what he might have found out, and she hoped he would share whatever it was with her. From now on, she wanted to know the truth, all of it. But she didn't intend to ask him what new information he'd uncovered. For now, she had enough readjustments to make, enough changes to accept. Nick and his work would have to wait until she was ready to take them on again.

She was as excited as a little girl at her school open house as she took Nick on a tour of her small apartment on the eight floor of the modern high-rise.

"The furniture is nothing special, but aren't the colors cheerful and nice?" she asked, anxious to hear his opinion. "And they gave me my choice of a vacancy with a view of Pearl Harbor, or one on this side, facing the mountains. Wait until you see the view of the Koolaus."

Nick stepped outside. "You have a nice long balcony."

"Oh, please. Don't call this a balcony, or a porch, or a terrace, Mr. New Yorker," she laughed with a feigned horror. "In Hawaii this is a *lanai*, if you please."

"Somehow anything said in Hawaiian is so much softer, and instantly more beautiful, don't you think?" he said, looking down at her in the darkness. "*Kilikina*," he said, softly rolling the word toward her, and she was surprised that he knew her name in Hawaiian.

Alone with him like this, in her own apartment with no strict protector to overhear, she was awed and a bit intimidated to realize that she had no excuses for avoiding him. She moved away, supposedly to adjust the placement of a wicker chair. She had thought he was about to put his arms around her, but he made no move to follow her, and she wondered if she had been wrong.

"So, do you like the place?" she asked.

"I think it's perfect for you. It's bright and open, and you can fix it up with all kinds of personal touches before long."

She felt braver, already adjusting to making her own decisions, to setting her own limits. Here in her eighth-floor hideaway, she would decide what she could take on and what she should avoid.

"I hope you'll come here often to visit," she said, so brazenly she surprised herself.

She wondered just how involved with Jenny he had become. Had he rushed the girl with the same amorous style of pursuit he'd employed with her? Did he tell her that her slender figure was gorgeous? Did he have any time left over for visits to a person who was no longer so useful to him?

Suddenly Nick turned stiffly and went inside, and she followed, wondering why he'd ignored her open invitation, making no comment on it at all.

He walked over to the door as if he were going to leave, and she began to think he was going to walk out of her life forever. Perhaps he had the same impression of finality, because he turned abruptly to her and looked her up and down as if he were memorizing what he was seeing for some future time. Then he looked around the room, scanning it, assessing it to make sure it was exactly what it should be. be.

"There's only one thing wrong with this new life of yours," he said at last. "I watched you hanging up all your drab old clothes in the closet and they just don't fit in here. Look at you. You could be a matron in the jail, dressed that way."

She looked down at her pearl gray blouse, worn with a chambray skirt of a darker gray. She had to agree with him.

"You can't dress that way in Hawaii," he said. "The first time you appeared at my hotel room door I thought you been dropped from outer space. I couldn't believe you liveᵤ here and dressed that way."

"Isn't that part of my charm?" she asked with a lilt to her voice. "To be different from all the other *wahinis*."

"Do you enjoy dressing that way?" he asked, for once failing to see any humor in the situation.

"No."

"Then be ready at two o'clock tomorrow afternoon. I've got to take you shopping. Someone has to drag you into the modern world. You spend the morning at the beach, working on that tan you've started."

After firing off these orders he turned and walked out her door, and if she felt any disappointment at his leaving so abruptly, she was compensated by her thoughts of what tomorrow would bring.

She twirled around in the center of her little living room, then stopped to hug her arms around herself.

There's so much to do. And it's all going to be so much fun.

She knew she had done the right thing in moving out of the Hanover house, making a clean psychological break with the past. She was flooded with an eager optimism, a love for whatever tomorrow might bring.

Then she began whistling to herself as she fumbled through her handbag, trying to find a notepad on which to list all the things she wanted to buy for her new home, and herself.

When Nick arrived at her apartment the next afternoon he chuckled as soon as he entered and saw her damp bathing suit stretched across a chair, her shoes kicked off in the middle of the room, and her breakfast dishes still on the table. By the time he peeked into her bedroom and saw her bed still rumpled and unmade he was laughing uncontrollably.

"I can't believe it. What a wonderful surprise," he said, wiping his eyes.

Christine started scurrying about to pick things up.

"No, don't touch a thing. I love your place this way," he said, still laughing. "You mean that all this time, inside that meticulous and precise person, there was a messy slob just waiting to burst forth?"

"I guess so," she said with a guilty giggle. "You told me I had to learn to relax."

"When you go loose on me, baby, you really come completely unglued," he said, throwing the wadded-up bathing suit across the room at her. "Now, can you get your act together enough to come shopping? Where shall we go? Ala Moana Shopping Center, King's Alley, Kilohana Square, Ward Warehouse, the International Market Place, uh, Kahala Mall, Pearlridge. This is a shopper's paradise."

"You certainly seem to know your way around. You must take a lot of ladies on shopping trips around Honolulu."

"Did it ever occur to you that I do a little shopping here for myself?" He ran his hands up and down his broad chest to call attention to the safari shirt he was wearing, obviously new and expensive. "It isn't easy to keep myself so well turned out."

Nick took her in and out of dozens of stores, where she wrote checks so fast she wondered how soon her conservative brother-in-law would cut off her allowance. When they returned to her apartment she had stacks of boxes and bags to unpack, and out came international treasures.

There were traditional Hawaiian prints, with patterns taken from the shapes found in island gardens, Oriental silks, and gauzy embroidered pieces from Thailand and the Philippines. The styles were neither stiff nor shapeless. Most were form-fitting, like the slinky Chinese cheongsam dress with a slit up one side, or the daringly low-cut purple sundress she'd worn home because she loved it so much. There was an airy voile with a deep elasticized ruffle around the top, meant to be worn off the shoulders. It was vivid pink, almost fuschia, and Nick especially liked that one.

She'd bought a holomuu, which was more form-fitting

than the traditional loose muu-muu, and a striking jade silk
that was a contemporary version of the wrapped Hawaiian
kikepa, with one shoulder left bare.

Tissue paper, hangers, and crumbled sacks littered the
floor as Nick stepped across the debris toward the door.

"All right. I've had enough. I've watched you try on
slacks and bikinis and bare midriff what-cha-ma-callits. I
can't look at one more piece of frou-frou. My eyes feel like
burned holes in a blanket!"

"You were awfully nice to go with me. I saw more than
one woman give me an envious look because I had someone
along telling me that everything I tried on looked swell and
I should buy it."

"Now where are you going to wear all these fine pretty
clothes?" he asked, a mocking expression coming over his
face.

She had never thought of that. "I don't know. I guess
I got a little carried away. I don't go out that much."

Looking at her disappointed face, he must have decided
to postpone his resolution to stay out of her life for just a
bit longer. "How about wearing that hot pink number tomorrow night? I know you can't wait to show it off. I'll
take you out to dinner. Be ready at eight."

After he had left, Christine had the disturbed feeling that
she'd bought all these new clothes with just this in mind:
wearing them out with Nick, basking in his admiring smiles
and the practiced flattery he knew how to use so well. If
he was manipulating her, if he was using her for his own
purposes, it didn't matter to her for the moment. She knew
only that she enjoyed his company, looked forward to seeing
him, and that she now had the wardrobe for any big plans
to see the sights of Honolulu that he might come up with.

The next morning Christine's doorbell sounded before
she'd even gotten out of bed. Because Nick was the only
one who knew her new address, she went to the door breath-
lessly, wondering what new adventure he'd thought up.

"Why, Jenny. What a surprise. How did you find me?"

"Nick gave me the address. Is it supposed to be a secret
or something? Are you hiding out from the family? That's

what Dad and Grandmother are beginning to think, you
know."

"I was going to call them both this morning and let them
know where I could be reached. Of course I'm not hiding
from anyone."

"Especially not from Nick Carruthers," Jenny said
snidely as she stepped inside. "He's been your only invited
guest so far, he tells me."

"Nick helped me move," Christine explained.

"It was a bit overdramatic, wasn't it, your hasty departure? When Grandmother summoned us this morning she
was in a completely distraught state. And Dad is speech-
less."

"I didn't think it would shock them so much. I am a
grown woman, and I've always wanted a place of my own,
close to my job."

"What do you mean, job?" Jenny said the word as if it
was something abhorrent to her. "You don't have to work.
Your late husband was a rich man, or hadn't you noticed?"

In spite of her best intentions to treat Jenny kindly, Christine was losing her patience. "If the family sent you to check
up on me, please tell them I am fine, and I'll visit them
later today so they can see for themselves."

"They think you've lost your mind, and they think Nick
is responsible. Have you been led astray, Mrs. Hanover?"

"What kind of question is that from a loving niece?"
Christine asked, her eyes narrowing with anger.

"You are to stop seeing Nick Carruthers."

"What?"

"There was a family conference this morning. It was
decided that you are no longer the proper person to guide
Mr. Carruthers' research efforts."

"Why, that's ridiculous."

"You were supposed to keep him on an even keel, make
sure he told his story correctly. Instead, you're following
after him as though he's some kind of Svengali. Dad says
that since you've left the family home, that's that. You
should also withdraw from this family project."

Christine was so confused that she grasped at the first

specific detail she could think of and blurted it out before she realized how irrelevant it was. "But I have a dinner date with Nick tonight."

"After that you must brush him off. Tell him this big job of yours is keeping you too busy. I'll drive him around to his interviews and things. Dad has asked me to keep an eye on him." The little nymph still in her teens was speaking with inflated self-importance. "He likes me, I can tell. He finds my island spirit very invigorating, he says. I can make sure his work turns out just fine. If you'll just butt out!"

Christine knew that she had never resisted anything Mrs. Hanover or Andrew had asked of her, so it was no wonder that they had felt no compunction at sending her these ridiculous orders. But they were not used to dealing with the new Christine, the emancipated woman who had untied herself from their domination.

"I am leading my own life now, Jenny. And making my own decisions."

With a sharp insight that must have been instinctive in one so young, Jenny swiftly regrouped her forces, and with glinting eyes brought out her big guns, moving them into firing position. The guilt would do it, she seemed confident.

"How can you do this to people who've been so kind to you? Is this any way to repay Grandmother's kindness to you? Why, Dad has told me how she's treated you just like a daughter these past few years, giving you a home, trusting you completely. And then you just walk out and leave her alone, turning your back on her on a moment's notice."

Christine sank into a chair, defeated. She knew she did owe the family loyalty, if not the total allegiance she'd given them until now. This book about her heroic son meant everything to Mrs. Hanover.

"And you think you can influence Nick's writings?"

"I'm going to use all the wiles I can think of," the girl said, giving her hips a flirty little twitch. "He needs the family's cooperation, and I intend to give it to him, but only up to a point. I don't lose my head just because a man shows me a little attention."

This spoiled child had always gotten everything she

wanted, and didn't see any reason why she wouldn't be able to manipulate the famous writer just as easily as she did her mother, father, grandmother, and all the adoring surfers who had kept her telephone ringing since she'd come to Hawaii.

"If this is what the family wants, then I'll stop seeing Nick," Christine said with a sagging feeling of still having one foot ensnared in a net of guilt feelings.

But Jenny wasn't ready to gracefully take her winnings and depart. "We think Nick saw you as the weak link in the chain. The one person in the family he could win over with his charm and flattery. And you seem to have fallen for it, but good," she said, looking around the apartment with the critical eye of her grandmother, as if she were examining the illicit love nest of a fallen woman.

Now that she had acquiesced, Christine wanted Jenny out of her place so she could be completely alone with her thoughts. She stood up and walked to the door.

"You have my agreement, now go home and tell everyone to breathe easily. I'll be too busy in the weeks ahead to give any more time to the project, anyway. I'll come by this afternoon and assure Mrs. Hanover of that."

"Don't bother. She's upset enough. Your presence would only remind her of what you've done. Just live up to this one last thing she's asking of you before you turn your back on the cause completely."

When Jenny had gone, Christine realized that everything was probably working out for the best. After tonight, she would not spend any more time alone with Nick. His attraction to her had been flattering, and because of it her courage to be her own person had been awakened. But now she needed time to adjust to the dizzying freedom. For the author, these recent days had been a vacation dalliance, a bit of amorous play in order to win an advantage he was looking for, and they would be quickly forgotten. But if she weren't careful, she could let her new and vibrant eagerness for life lead her into a hopeless attachment to the man who had liberated her.

CHAPTER SIX

WHEN NICK ARRIVED that evening she wasn't dressed yet. It had taken her more time than she'd thought it would to clean up the apartment and put things in place, including the new capiz-shell wind chimes she'd bought yesterday for the lanai and the bright round tapa-cloth circle dyed in the ancient native fashion that she'd found for her living room wall.

She answered the door wrapped in her old print kimono.

"You're not ready yet? Christine Hanover is late! Well, now I know that the metamorphosis is complete." As she turned to rush for the bedroom he gave her a comradely spank on her bottom. "Hurry up, we have reservations."

Alone in her room she studied her face in the mirror. She needed very little makeup, for the brief hours spent in the sun at Nick's instruction yesterday had added an amazing amount of luster to her skin. By contrast, or because it too had been changed by the sun, her brown hair seemed lighter, almost a dappled blond. She reached for her hair pins, then dropped them, deciding to wear her freshly washed hair long and flowing. She slipped into the hot-pink voile dress, tugged the neckline low on her shoulders, and went to show Nick, knowing already that her transformation was dazzling.

"My God," he said after a wolfish whistle when he saw her. "You look better than I expected, and that's saying a lot. I promised myself I wouldn't touch you, but I can't resist."

He held out his arms toward her, and she was surprised to find herself moving into them quite naturally. But there was a hitch to her breath, showing her excited anticipation as his arms enfolded her.

"I fully intended to give you some time. I didn't want to rush you like this. But I can't keep my hands off of you."

He was speaking close to her ear, and the hot flame of his breath felt more dangerous and overpowering than the fire she'd walked into that afternoon not long ago. "You are gorgeous, do you know that?"

He kissed her with a lingering appreciation, as if he wanted to savor every moment of it. His long fingers went to her hair, and he used them like giant combs, raking loose the wavy mass she had finally unleashed. Then his hands stopped at the back of her neck, and he held on to her as tightly as if he were keeping a drowning woman's head above water. She did feel as if he had saved her, as if he had given her this new start, this chance to sample the brilliant and confusing world where there were no longer any external controls upon her behavior. And now he was leading her through it, showing her how to appreciate the freedom.

When at last he drew away from her she looked up into his eyes, where fires were slowly burning down into sapphire stillness, and she felt an uneasy longing. Would the future be as glorious without him? Or had he become an indispensable part of her new life?

She gave a too-hearty shrug, a self-conscious laugh, and said, "Come on. Let's see some of this Honolulu nightlife you think is so great."

He took her to the Rainbow Bazaar at the Hilton Hawaiian Village Hotel, and they had dinner at the old Japanese inn that had been transplanted there and now served as the Benihana Restaurant.

Their table had a hibachi grill built right into the center of it. After they'd ordered their sukiyaki steaks, a sinister-looking fellow with the drooping mustache of a samurai warrior—and a gleaming knife in his hand to complete the impression—came to their table and began putting on a show for them. He wore the high white hat of a chef on his head and his act became quite humorous as his whirling knife slipped through the air, slicing the huge steak into precise, even slices and the vegetables into artistic dice. He cooked their dinners for them as they watched, moving the food about on the sizzling metal surface expertly, releasing the aroma of the mysterious spices he applied with a flourish from a blue-glazed pitcher. All the while he kept up a pidgin-English patter that had them both laughing with amusement.

Christine wondered if Nick had paid a huge tip in order to get such a performance, but then she noticed the same thing happening at the tables all around them. When each dinner was served, the circle of guests around the hibachi usually broke into a round of applause for their very theatrical cook.

After they'd eaten every bite, and enjoyed a cup of tea, Nick suggested they stroll through the shops and out to the beach in front of the hotel.

"Take off your shoes, and let's walk in the sand," he suggested, and they began a romantic odyssey through the embracing air of a Honolulu night, with the sounds of the surf pounding in the darkness on one side of them and the musical throbbings from the nightclub shows at the various hotels they were passing on the other side of them.

They walked for a long time in silence. Then with the black night as a shield, Christine found the nerve to say to Nick, "I've been thinking a lot about what you told me the other day about David. I mean about his actions on that last mission."

Nick started to interrupt her and she stopped him, pausing in the deep sand around her ankles to turn and face him. "No, I don't want to hear any more evidence about it one way or another. Whether it happened the way you say or not, I don't care. You've made me consider the possibility, and that's enough. I remember things more clearly now. I'm viewing the past realistically."

He brushed the hair back from her face, for the soft

evening breeze was billowing it around her. Then he said, "I didn't mean to be cruel, destroying your illusions about David. I only wanted you to stop living in the past. If I've accomplished that, I'm glad."

She looked up at him, drinking in her impressions of this night and this man she might never be close to again. The remembrance of Jenny's warning to stay away from him pained her, for it meant that some of the most delicious pleasures of her new life were being taken away from her. She would not get to look into those gem-hard eyes with their softening halo of thick dark eyelashes; she would not get to touch that dark hair that surged through her fingers when she touched it like moving waves across the ocean. There would only be evenings alone, silent telephone bells, tables for one, solitary walks on the beach.

Nick looked down, sensing her melancholy mood even if there was no way he could understand it. He took one finger and ran it lightly across first one cheekbone and then the other, as if trying by magic to read her thoughts.

He kissed her bare shoulders, and her neck, and she gave a light laugh in response. Then her contented sounds were stilled as he found her lips and she responded to him with an ardency that surprised them both. She'd never known this anxious desire to return to her partner every moment of satisfaction he was giving her. Nick's kisses had an effect on her unlike any she'd ever known, and she greedily absorbed the sensations, knowing she might never taste them again. He didn't know it, but she was well aware: there was only tonight.

Some passers-by on the beach startled them, and they reluctantly pulled their bodies away from each other and began walking again, hand in hand. Christine knew that it was only natural to feel an infatuation for Nick, and she was sure it would pass away soon enough. After all, he'd been the catalyst who had brought tremendous changes in her life, and she had reasons to be grateful to him.

She also had a purely physical attraction to him that could not be denied. But that was easily explainable too. She hadn't been held or kissed by a man in years, and she was hungry for the presence of a masculine body close to hers. Just the touch of his hand as it held hers loosely while they walked was enough to draw her powers of concentration to the point where their skin made contact until she found herself flushed and breathing hard, imagining the same strong hand at her throat, upon her breasts, or down her bare back.

But, she assured herself, all these annoying preoccupations would soon be gone. During the weeks ahead she would not see him, and soon she would forget all about him. She would not want him . . . after tonight.

"You know, I'm tired of hearing all the expensive floor shows from way out here like a beach bum. Let's go back to the Halekulani and have a drink and watch the show."

"Well . . ." Christine hesitated. She found it hard to believe that anything could be more enjoyable than strolling through the night with Nick.

"I'll buy you one of those coconut drinks I was telling you about," he coaxed.

"You're hard to resist," she said, affirming the truth of that statement in the depths of her heart. "I'll race you!"

"You little devil," he gasped as she shot away from him down the beach. But with his long legs, he'd soon caught up with her and was flying along just beside her, where the flounces of her light skirt often blew against his knees as they laughed and ran.

If the person she'd been just two weeks ago were watching her tonight, hair flying in a tangle, racing along the beach through curious clumps of tourists, a laughing man at her heels trying to grab her, she would have been scandalized. How different the two Christines were. And yet how quickly and easily the happier one had been released. Christine knew one thing for sure: she could never return to being that obedient and docile soul the Hanovers had controlled like a puppet.

When they stopped to put on their shoes outside the hotel, Christine used the last few moments of quiet and privacy to say what she'd been working up to all evening.

"Nick, I have to ask you one more favor. I want you to stop this work on your book and leave Hawaii."

He stopped what he was doing to stare at her with astonishment.

"Is that really what you want?"

"I don't think you realize how your book will damage the Hanover family's well-guarded reputation. It could ruin what's left of Mrs. Hanover's life, and it certainly will hurt Andrew's banking career."

"And what about you?"

"What I want is for you to consider the feelings of the Hanovers and leave them alone."

"And leave Hawaii?"

"Well, yes, there'd be no point . . ."

"You make it sound so easy."

"It should be a simple matter for you to find another subject for your next book."

"And forget all about the Hanovers."

"Yes, exactly."

"And you'd be glad to see the last of me, is that it?"

"Yes, well, no." She felt flustered, trying to make light of emotions that ran deeply within her. "Of course, I'll always remember your kindness in helping me, in giving me the courage to make the break."

"My kindness," he reiterated flatly.

"You've done so much for me; it's hard to make this additional request. But will you consider what I've said?"

"Oh, I'll give it a lot of consideration, believe me."

Christine had the uncomfortable feeling that she had somehow mishandled this delicate assignment. She had hoped that her open and honest approach might make Jenny's devious plan unnecessary. With hope high in her heart she had planned to gain his cooperation so that she could go right on seeing him, the family happy and satisfied with the results of her relationship with the writer.

But Christine did not enjoy asking more of a person than she had a right, couldn't think of clever ways to exert her will. She'd made the request outright, but Nick seemed to be seeing more to it than was there. There was a dark and brooding look on his face that disturbed her, and he certainly had not given her any quick assurances that he would agree to her proposal. Oh, well, she'd made a try, for the sake of her family loyalty. The more difficult sacrifice would come later, when she would refuse to see him any more. If he even asked her to, that is.

Perhaps, after all, it would be better to leave the persuasion in the cool and unemotional hands of little Jenny, she thought. She had more of an interest in game-playing and using people. Apparently she was conscience-free when it came to exploiting these talents.

She followed meekly behind Nick as he walked rapidly ahead of her into the hotel to the Coral Lanai, where a show was just about to begin. They found a table and he ordered them drinks, but he said not another word to her and she was glad when the dancers came out onto the stage and the music began, for the strange new distance between them was giving her wrenching feelings of regret for having spoken out as she did.

Christine had read about Marlene and Beverly Noa, but now she marveled at their artistry as they presented authentic Hawaiian dances, with the men of Na Kamalei to back them up. After one spectacular number with flaming torches tossed through the air, Christine looked toward Nick, trying to show him how impressed she was by what she was seeing. But as she clapped exuberantly, he sat stonily facing her, making no sign that he was enjoying himself.

Later, during a swelling love song, she turned to watch him. The brightly colored lights of the stage were reflected on the harsh planes of his face, but they gave only a garish kind of ghostliness to his empty expression. When he turned and caught her staring at him, she found that she reacted with an automatic smile.

She found a joyous satisfaction in studying the perfect symmetry of his features. His dominant chin, regal nose, and the aristocratic angle at which he tipped his head to one side. But the lack of warmth in his eyes when he returned her look wiped the happy look from her face almost at once, and she turned back to watching the performance on the stage, a little less enthusiastic for having no one to share the fun with.

"It's getting late, and I have work to do tomorrow," he said as soon as the show was over. "Do you want another drink?"

The invitation was such an uninterested afterthought that she quickly declined and began to gather up her things to leave.

"No, I guess we should be going," she said.

The drive back to her apartment was quiet, with Nick giving an unusual amount of care to his driving and Christine staring out the window to watch the sliver of moon as it followed them home. He walked her to her door with the polite detachment of a disappointed blind date after an evening arranged by a meddling aunt. When she'd opened the door she turned with surprise to see him hesitating in the hall.

"I won't come in with you," he said.

"Oh, come on. I'll make you a cup of Kona coffee. That's the least I can do after you've given me such a fine introduction to the culture of my own hometown."

Then she began to chatter about the beauty of the beach at night, the haunting quality that made Hawaiian music so evocative, and the crazy antics of the Japanese chef. As she did so, Nick came inside almost reluctantly and then followed her to the kitchen, where he watched without comments as she filled the coffee pot and put it on the stove.

"Shall we sit on the lanai while we're waiting for it to perk?" she asked with forced cheerfulness.

"Whatever you want," he said, and his distance numbed her.

When she was almost to the doorway outside she stopped to turn off the living room lights so that they could look out at the view without glare behind them. She heard the bounding motion of fast steps behind her, and just as the room was plunged into darkness, she felt Nick grab her from behind and twirl her about into his arms with a fury that took her breath away. For one terrifying moment she thought he was about to strike her or otherwise harm her, such was the tension in his muscular arms and the heaviness of his breathing. But she melted into his arms when she realized he was going to reward her with the kiss she had been waiting for since they left the beach.

This kiss was different, however, from all his others. It was not meant to tantalize but to overpower. He almost smothered her lips with his demanding mastery, and he clawed through the feathery fabric of her dress to painfully scratch at the sunburn on her back as he clasped her tightly, almost punishingly, against him.

But even this new and more compelling Nick was exciting to her senses, and she twisted in his arms, working in concert with him to elevate every sensation to its utmost effect. If only she could go on like this forever, reveling in his embrace. If only Jenny's heavy dose of guilt hadn't had its effect upon her, reviving her still-present sense of duty. If she had her choice she would spend every moment she could with Nick while he was here, indulging herself in these rare and exotic pleasures. Her hands sought his face, and the caress of her trembling fingers demonstrated her desperation to experience all that he had to offer before it was too late.

She felt Nick pull at the ruffled neckline of her dress, felt the insistent brazenness of the gesture as he bared her breasts to the roughly stimulating exploration of his hands. She gave an ecstatic sigh that she was powerless to withhold, and her response seemed to anger rather than entice him. His next kiss was almost abusive in effect, lacking in any consciousness of his partner's comfort. He ignored the thrilling shudder of pain she gave as he pulled away.

"You've turned into quite a little femme fatale," he whispered thickly.

Christine gave a throaty attempt at a laugh, the rising tingling feeling inside of her obliterating any attempt to consider the meaning of his words.

"I guess you've bottled up these feelings for a long time," he said.

"Almost forever," she murmured.

"Saved them until you really needed them."

"Nick, I've never felt this way before."

"Well, you certainly have a knack for it." He released his brutal hold on her, disappointing her as he drew away. "You seem to know just how to use your feminine charms to get what you want."

"I don't understand what you mean."

"I mean you're trying every trick you can think of to win me over; you're trying to make me forget what it is I came here to do."

"No, I'm not." Her mind reeled with the confusing turn of his mood. She reached up and pulled her dress into place, suddenly embarrassed beneath his insulting look of disapproval.

"What else am I to think? You kiss me like that right after telling me that you'd just as soon I leave Hawaii. It's obvious your heart is not in this."

"This has nothing to do with what I said before," she stammered with a sudden feeling of outrage.

"We'll just see about that. I'll bet you'll be less anxious to croon in my arms when I tell you that I have no intention of stopping my work on this book. I plan to go right ahead with my interviews and my research. And I'm going to write just what I want to write. So, put away your collection of medals. You won't want them by the time I'm through."

"Why, you selfish, arrogant . . ."

"Watch it!" He grabbed her wrist before her hand could fly out to strike him as she probably would have. "See, I told you your passions would turn cold rather rapidly. Now that you're not going to get what you want, I'm not going to get what I want, either. Is that the deal?"

"What do you think I am?" she demanded.

"I think you are a fiercely protective woman. Just as devious as that self-righteous mother-in-law of yours, trying to throw me off the track. She knows very well what her son was like, just as you have known all along what your husband was like."

"No, I didn't remember any of it. I had buried it all."

"And you're both willing to do anything to perpetuate the lie, to keep the world believing that your devotion is not misplaced. That's false pride, Christine, and though you pretend you've thrown it over, tonight you've proved to me that it still motivates everything you do."

"You're wrong. You are so wrong." She felt she might burst into tears, but she bit into her lower lip to hold back the flow.

"Your little performance did not work. Tomorrow morning I'm through with shopping trips and leading forlorn little ladies on tours of the city. I'm getting back to work."

"And you can get right back to your willing assistant, Jenny. I don't intend to give you a minute more of my help. You and your filthy yellow journalism. I will not be a part of what you're trying to do."

"That's fine with me," he said. And his voice was so loud that she was glad she was now living in her own apartment or Mrs. Hanover would surely have come charging down the hall with a lecture on good manners.

"I'm sick and tired of your phony attentiveness and your inch-deep flattery," she said. "You've only been nice to me so that you could get information for your book."

Christine was now convinced that he had planned to lull her into the open and relaxed mood of a summer flirtation just so she would be inclined to speak recklessly to him and reveal any secrets she might know. Why, if this evening had progressed the way she thought it might, right at this moment she might be murmuring pillowtalk to him, confiding all kinds of material about her relationship with her former husband. To build Nick's ego, she might have confessed to him the stark lovelessness of her first marriage, David's boorish disinterest in her sexual fulfillment; she might have extolled the raptures she'd only learned recently, of having a skillful lover coax hungry desires from her that she thought herself incapable of ever having. She was that close to telling him everything, to sharing every important thought she'd ever had with him.

Nick was standing stock still, his anger having left whitened half-moon patches on each side of his mouth. "No matter what you think of my writing, you can't believe that I'd do that. That I would *use* you."

"I do believe it!" she proclaimed, wanting to add that the realization was causing her a great deal more sorrow than it could ever cause his unfeeling heart.

"Is that how little you think of yourself? Can't you believe that I was sincerely attracted to you? And I mean long before you came up with this crazy plan to throw yourself at me so blatantly."

"I did not throw myself at you, tonight or ever."

"You didn't have to do much," he said, lowering his eyes. "I'll have to admit I was always ready and willing," he said.

She remembered just how willing he had been, starting with their first meeting, to accuse her of having too much self-control, of repressing too much. All he had ever wanted was to loosen her up, gain her confidence, get her tongue moving. He had radically changed her life, and for what? Just for his own purposes.

"Get out," she charged toward him with her command, but her words were unnecessary, for he already had his hand on the doorknob and was ready to leave.

"Just one last word of warning, Chris. You should never tell a journalist to stop snooping into your life. It only makes him more curious than ever."

And with that sinister comment he was gone.

Christine went into the kitchen to silence the grumbling coffee pot which was belching up overcooked coffee onto the white enamel stove. How dare he threaten her like that? Just what else did this red-hot investigative reporter think he was going to ferret out? He had already decided David was a one-man Navy disaster, and had probably figured out that as a husband he was a faithless philanderer. There was no more mischief Nick could cause, she was certain of that. And so it was too late; there was no point in alarming Andrew now as to what was in store for them when the book was published. The worst had already happened.

Andrew obviously had serious misgivings about starting this project, and had enlisted Jenny's aid in controlling it. Now let that ambitious girl do what she could to stop the disaster from occurring. After all, it was time for Jenny to do her father a favor; she'd kept him worried and on edge ever since her unexpected arrival on his doorstep.

The thought of Jenny brought an ironic twist to her lips. Jenny was the one who had planned to use her coquetry to influence Nick, and Christine felt repulsed by the idea. But now here she stood, cruelly accused of that very same deceit by Nick himself.

She dabbed the sponge over the stove.

Oh, Nick, Nick, Nick. How could you think such a thing? Are you so blind and unreasonable that you see me that way? How could you accuse me of that kind of duplicity?

Then she threw the sponge aside with the job unfinished, and strode into the living room.

Thank goodness she wasn't in love with Nick Carruthers! Throwing off this girlish crush would be easy. After his terrible words to her this evening, she had no more tender feelings toward the man. She owed him nothing, all debts were off, and she could go on and pursue her exciting new life unencumbered by this senseless attraction. She had a brand-new wardrobe to wear, and she'd find places to wear it. She had five Hawaiian islands to explore. And she had a job that challenged her every day.

"Who could ask for anything more?" she sang, just a bit off tune, as she slipped off her shoes, kicked them under a chair, and headed for her bedroom to undress.

CHAPTER SEVEN

Is IT REALLY necessary that I make another trip to Pensacola? Well, it's lucky I've just hired a brand-new screener. We have a mess of referrals here and she can process them while I'm gone." Kim winked at Christine over the receiver as she wound up her long-distance telephone call.

"Pete is going to die when he hears this," she said, hanging up. "Just when he gets a two-week leave, I'm off on another trip."

"He can probably rearrange his duty schedule."

"I hope so. We rarely get together these days, since we're both so busy."

"I know that's hard, but I think you two have a wonderful marriage. You're both involved in things that are important to you in the outside world, and when you do get time off together, you have meaningful things to share. I envy you, Kim," Christine said.

"Yes, we appreciate those times when we can be together. Because they're so rare, they're very precious."

She stood up and looked out of the window of her barracks office. "But all my relatives keep asking us why I haven't got a big *opu* yet," she said, patting her stomach. "You know, why I'm not pregnant. And my mama tells them it's *a'ole hiki*, impossible, because she thinks we're never together." She shook her head with amusement, sending her straight dark hair swinging about her ears.

"People used to ask David and me why we didn't have children," Christine said softly.

Kim was a good enough friend not to pry by asking the obvious question. She merely turned to smile at Christine and let her know she could talk about it if she wanted to.

"David didn't want them. But he covered that up by making a lot of jokes about Navy life, long sea duty and all that."

"Very funny," Kim said sarcastically.

"He said when he was home he wanted me all to himself; he didn't want to share me with a bunch of kids."

"Look, I never knew your late, great husband, Christine. But from what little you've let slip about the man, I kind of get the impression he was a veritable tower of immaturity."

"Yes, I suppose in a way you're right," she said, thinking about that for just a moment, before she shook herself loose from the morbid post-mortems and turned back to the more productive topic of her work. "I heard you say on the phone that you have a lot for me to do. Shall we get to it?"

"I don't want to scare you on your first day as a professional here."

"Load it on, boss. That's what I'm here for."

"Here are the folders on the new men you'll be interviewing. You can read over their health and service records this morning, and then we can start scheduling the appointments."

"And while you're gone I'm to decide which ones need NASAP?" Christine asked with awe.

"Yes. Try to separate out those who are simply alcohol 'misusers' and need our help, from those who are alcohol 'abusers' and should have more intensive treatment, like the two-week drydock program. What we're looking for is the boy who's gotten in trouble for the first time because of drinking—maybe a drunk driving arrest, some kind of brawl while on liberty, an accident that happens on duty which his CO reports."

"Then we put them through this thirty-six-hour class and

try to prevent their becoming dependent on alcohol in the future."

"Exactly. We do that by offering them positive role models, changing their attitudes toward drinking so they leave here believing it is socially acceptable to choose not to drink. We want to change that old image of the sailor as a hard-drinking troublemaker."

"You're leaving me with a big responsibility my first week."

"There'll still be an Officer in Charge in case you run into problems. And I'll review all your decisions when I return. I'm sure glad you've decided to work here on a regular basis and get paid for it at last."

"Well, even though I'm only working three days a week, I'll probably keep coming in as a volunteer the other two days. I love this program. If my mother had been offered something like this, she might still be alive."

"A lot of us are here for personal reasons, Christine. We're helping here because there was someone we wanted to help, and couldn't."

Christine picked up the towering stack of papers and headed out of Kim's office toward her little screening room.

Kim stopped her. "By the way. You had a couple of phone messages before you came in."

"Already?"

"Your mother-in-law left orders for you to check in with her. And that very attractive man I saw you with, Nick Carruthers, called. Both of them said you weren't answering your phone at the apartment."

"No, I wasn't," Christine said, taking the message slips and crumpling them both in her hand. Then she saw Kim's quizzical smile. "I'd better get to work. We'll talk at lunch, if you're available."

"You bet I am," Kim laughed. "My curiosity is killing me. I can see that you've made a lot of changes in your life lately, and I want to hear all about them."

"You will."

Christine was eager to get at the stack of personnel folders. Until now her work at NASAP has been mainly filing and office work while she learned the procedures. Now she would be working in close contact with the men and women referred to the program. It was exciting to think that she was in a position to influence people's futures, help them improve their chances for success in the Navy and in their personal lives. She became so absorbed in her work during the morning that she was able to forget all about the phone calls she didn't want to return.

She had remained incommunicado for the past four or five days, enjoying the hours alone to put her new apartment in order and taking time out now and then to explore her new neighborhood. Not far from her apartment, about three miles up Aiea Heights Road, she had found there was a lovely state park that contained the ruins of Keaiwa Heiau, the ancient healing temple. It was peaceful to walk among the Norfolk pines there and the plants grown by the early Hawaiians for medicinal purposes.

Christine was happy to find out that having unstructured time to herself was not the least bit depressing, and that doing things alone felt adventurous. She was never at a loss for something to do; there seemed to be a list four pages long in the back of her mind of natural wonders she had heard about on the island of Oahu but never had an opportunity to visit.

There was one piece of unfinished business, however, that was unpleasant and had to be performed. So one day, upon returning from a meditative walk in the park, she placed the dreaded phone call to Florence Hanover that she had been avoiding.

After a moment or two of forced pleasantries, and inquiring with real interest into the woman's health and her social life, Christine said, "I'm sure you're keeping busy, even without me to accompany you everywhere. I know you'll want to go right on doing that Navy Relief work, and you have lots of friends who would meet you for lunch at the O Club, if you'd only take the trouble to call them and make a date."

"I just don't understand why you've abandoned me,

Christine. Even if you've moved out, I should think you could drive over here once in a while and take me somewhere."

"I plan to do that, Mrs. Hanover, very soon. But I'm busy getting settled in my new place, and soon I'll have my job to keep me tied up."

"What exactly is this No-Cap you're going to work for?"

"It's NASAP. You heard me talk about it when I was a volunteer there."

"How will I explain to people why you've taken a job for money? It will make it seem that your husband didn't leave you properly taken care of," Mrs. Hanover complained. "You said it's a Navy project, at least. You're not becoming a social worker or something like that?"

"No, I'll be working for the Navy."

"Well, the idea of your working at all is ridiculous! You'll have no time at all for hair appointments, or shopping, or bridge games, or any of the things you used to do with me."

It was hard to disguise the sigh of relief that slipped into her answer. "No, I won't."

"I don't know, Christine. Andrew and I disapprove of this careless new lifestyle of yours. What would David think if he were still here?"

"But he isn't here, is he?"

"I think you've forgotten all about my boy. You've probably forgotten that there's to be a Change of Command ceremony on his destroyer next Saturday, and that you said you would attend it."

"I haven't forgotten. Now, if you'll excuse me," Christine said, swallowing the lump in her throat, "I have to go to the laundry room and retrieve a load of clothes from the dryer."

"The what? Where are you going?"

"Goodbye, Mrs. Hanover."

Duties, responsibilities, family ties—when did they ever end? Or did she want to sever them completely? But how could she reestablish contact with the Hanovers ever again without being swallowed up by them? During the following days she had contemplated all that.

"Telephone call for you, Mrs. Hanover." A First Class Corpsmen peeked in her office door, interrupting her work reading the files. "It's the senior Mrs. Hanover, ma'am."

Christine looked at her watch. She didn't want to pick up that last phone conversation right now.

"Can you tell her I've already left for lunch? It's after twelve."

"Yes, ma'am. I told her I'd go look for you. I'll just say you're on your way to lunch."

"And I'll get going right now so we won't make a liar of you."

"Thank you, ma'am," he said with a youthful seriousness.

Christine stretched her arms over her head to reduce the fatigue of a long morning's work. Just then Kim came down the hall into her office.

"What's this I hear about lunch?" Kim asked. "Are you ready to go?"

"I sure am. I think I've done three day's work this morning." She laughed at her own industriousness.

"Well, you deserve a little celebration after such an auspicious beginning to your first paid employment. I'm taking you to lunch. I asked the Corpsman to call and reserve us a table at the Pearl City Tavern."

Christine stood up and smoothed her skirt. Kim leaned against the doorjamb watching her with envious amusement.

"We have to go someplace special for lunch, since you're so beautifully decked out today. I love your new dress."

Christine was wearing a rose print halter-top dress with a short raspberry-colored jacket over it. It was one of the outfits Nick had picked out.

"Are you trying to look like a young girl or something?" Kim teased.

As they walked to the car Christine continued the conversation. "You know, it's amazing. The clothes you wear have an effect on your feelings."

"The military figured that out many centuries ago," Kim said with a laugh. "That's why they thought up uniforms, so that everyone would know his place."

"Well, I'm sure glad to be out of my old drab uniforms."

Christine drove through the Nimitz Gate, which was right across from their old barracks office, and out onto Kamehameha Highway, which would take them around the East Loch of Pearl Harbor to the Pearl City Tavern, lovingly called the P.C.T. by the locals.

They passed through the bar, stopping to watch the dozen or so squirrel monkeys cavorting in the glass cages behind the bartenders, then went to their tables in the Oriental-style dining room. They were both hungry, and they ordered clam chowder, the shrimp tempura the place was famous for, and green tea.

While they sat waiting to eat, Kim buoyed up Christine's confidence concerning the responsible new job she was undertaking. "You have nothing to worry about. The most important thing we ask our screeners is to maintain a warm, accepting attitude. They are the first of our people the new client meets, and they should give that nervous or hostile sailor the impression that he is welcome and he is important. This is the moment when he can start feeling good about himself. I know you well enough to know you'll do just fine at that."

As they drank their soup, Christine brought her friend up to date on her new apartment and the touchy situation of extricating herself from her time-consuming schedule of commitments to Mrs. Hanover. She carefully avoided the topic that was keeping an expectant expression on her friend's face until she happened to look up across the room and blurt out, "Why, there's Nick Carruthers."

"Well, at last we're getting around to the subject I came to hear about. The new man in your life."

"There's no man in my life."

"Oh, are your cheeks turning such a bright shade of pink just to match your new dress?"

Christine didn't answer, for she was staring across the dining room at the tall man who had just come in to speak to the kimono-clad hostess. Then she noticed that Jenny had come up behind Nick and was possessively attaching herself to his arm as they waited for a table.

Kim turned around in her chair to look. "Maybe if you'd returned his call he wouldn't have come looking for you."

"He isn't looking for me. Is he?"

"He's looking all around the room. And the office does know where we are. If he called there again, they might have told him where we'd gone for lunch."

"My niece Jenny has been taking him to a lot of appointments on the base. They probably just came here by chance."

"Oh yeah? Then why is he making a beeline straight to our table?"

Watching Nick come toward her, Christine could identify with the feelings her young clients were going to encounter when they were first faced with the offer to "Have a few beers," after going through her training program. She had sworn off Nick Carruthers, and drawing on those old and well-practiced habits of mental discipline she had closed him out of her thoughts for these past few days. But watching him come toward her, she wanted to hide under the table. She wasn't sure she was strong enough yet to withstand the temptation of being near him.

"Is this a working lunch, or may we join you for a moment?" Nick asked, pulling out one of the extra chairs at their table for Jenny and then settling himself in the other one. "You ladies no doubt have work matters to discuss, so we'll keep this brief."

Kim was able to find her tongue before Christine, and she said, "No, sit down and join us, by all means."

"Have you met Christine's niece, Jenny Hanover?" Nick asked Kim, avoiding Christine's clouded eyes. "Jenny, this is Kim Malone, Christine's supervisor in the alcoholism program."

Jenny did not seem impressed. "Hi, Kim," she said with a bored look.

Christine had forgotten the dynamic vitality that Nick Carruthers exuded. His masterful dominance clearly pre-

sided over the three women at the table, if not all the rest
of the people in the room, or the millions of the world.
Christine had not let herself believe that his absence from
her life during the last few days had been an important one.
She had been too intent upon learning to love her new life,
coming to grips with the heady independence, and the exhilaration of making it on her own. But now, sitting again
beside him, the musky male perfume of his skin close
enough to reach out and sample with a quick nuzzle if she'd
let herself, she was struck by feelings of loss.

The sound of his voice speaking the polite words of social
introduction brought back the remembrance of soft words
uttered close to her ear. A glimpse of his large hands twisting
a fork round and round between his fingers to release his
boundless energy made her yearn for his hands once again
to be spreading coconut lotion all over her body.

"Aren't you going to give Grandmother an answer?"
came a sing-song question in her direction, pulling her from
her trance.

"I'm sorry, Jenny. An answer to what?"

"Grandmother has been trying and trying to reach you.
She's almost going crazy. She keeps tracking down Nick
and me wherever we are to complain about you, Christine,
and it's becoming a bore. Whether we're at work or at play,
we're constantly being interrupted. Why, once she even had
us paged at the beach, remember Nicky? Finally, this darling
man said he'd had enough, that he was going to find you
and get an answer for Grandmother one way or the other."

Nick reached out and grasped Jenny's arm, either to
silence her prattling or more likely because he'd grown
accustomed to this easy and affectionate manner with her.

"Florence claims she doesn't know if you'll show up for
this Change of Command ceremony that you're supposed
to attend, Christine." He spoke with slow patience, as if he
had become used to speaking to a child.

"Of course I'm planning to be there. I accepted that
invitation a long time ago, and I will attend," she told him.

"Daddy says he just doesn't know what to expect from
you any more. He says you were twenty minutes late get-

ting dressed for a date with him the other night," Jenny said.

Nick gave Christine a smugly superior smile, as if to say he had predicted that she and Andrew would soon become an unbreakable twosome. "Did you have a nice time, once you finally got yourself organized?" he asked her.

"I'd never seen Danny Kaleikini's show, and Andrew hadn't either, so I dragged him to it. I think he enjoyed it."

"Why, Mrs. Hanover," he laughed. "The next thing we know we may find you sitting on ti leaves on the sand, eating kalua pig, salt fish, and lomi-lomi salmon at some luau, and getting up to dance a hula for the crowd. You and Andrew seem to be 'going native' after all this time."

Christine was hurt that he would make her the object of his cruel jests in public.

"Ugh! Anything would be better than those dumb hotel shows," Jenny said with girlish frankness. "Only middle-aged tourists go there."

Kim could take no more of Jenny's blithe insults. She bought all her bikinis at the shop owned by Danny Kaleikini's wife and was a personal friend of hers. "Danny is a very talented musician, and his show is well attended by *kamaainas* who know the authentic music of . . ."

The girl didn't know enough to be the least bit daunted by the opinion of one older and more expert in these matters. "Nick and I are going to a place where they play slack-key guitar tonight, aren't we?" she cooed into her companion's face. "We've been out every night this week. Nick says I'm tireless."

Christine could see that the girl's plan was working, for Nick seemed to be too occupied with this bustling social schedule to have much time left over to worry about the book he'd come here to write.

Jenny jumped to her feet, having given all the messages she'd come to impart, not the least important of which was the clear-cut signal to Christine that she had everything firmly in her control where Nick was concerned.

"Come on, Nick. We've found her and gotten our answer for Grandmother. Let's go."

"I think my friend is giving me the hint that she'd like to go get something to eat. See you later," Nick said, getting up to follow her.

Kim mumbled under her breath, "Children do have to be fed on time or they get very cranky, don't they?"

When Christine did not give her any reaction in reply, she tried again. "I think he should have left that nasty child in the other room to watch the monkeys play."

"Hmm?"

"I'm certainly glad there's no man in your life to get you all distracted and hard to talk to. It's nice having your complete attention like this, Chris. Now, shall we eat? Here's your fork; you just move it like this across your plate."

Christine was finally able to smile at her friend, but during the rest of the meal she had little to say.

On Saturday morning Andrew called to offer Christine a ride to the military ceremony, but she declined, since he had Jenny and his mother to worry about already. She had to keep assuring him that she would be on time and that she would dress appropriately. Apparently the last time he'd seen her, dressed in her jade-green backless silk, and not as punctual as usual, he had become aware that the disturbing rebelliousness in her ran deep and was not just a midsummer madness that would soon disappear.

To satisfy him, she put on one of her old dresses, a short-sleeved brown cotton twill coatdress that fastened all the way up the front to her chin with covered buttons. It depressed her to look in the mirror, remembering how long she had kept her figure disguised in this kind of dress. She was already becoming accustomed to the whistles and cat calls that greeted her every stroll around the Navy base. And she wondered how she could have survived that long confinement of her spirit, when no one knew what she was really like.

The U.S.S. Brewster was pulled up alongside the Sea Landing for the day's festivities, and as Christine hurried up the portable stairway that was rolled up on the dock next to it, the men of the crew snapped to attention, saluting her respectfully. No matter what these men who had served under him thought of her husband's command, they had always treated her with friendliness and courtesy. It was easier for her, though, to react to them openly and honestly now that she wasn't trying to bury all her doubts and suspicions about her husband's career. She had faced the truth, and discarded it as unimportant to her life now. She was here today to honor the new commanding officer of the *Brewster*, and the one departing to take a staff job in Washington. David's role in all of this was irrelevant today.

"Mrs. Hanover, I'll escort you to the rest of your party."

A starched and polished Lieutenant led her to the forward deck, where a band was lined up along the starboard side. Mrs. Hanover and Andrew were seated on folding chairs amidst a covey of military brass looking proudly comfortable, and Christine went to take the empty chair they pointed out to her.

As if in accompaniment, the band struck up its first march of the day just as Nicolas Carruthers appeared on deck. Jenny was beside him, dressed in a saucy print with a full skirt that tended to catch every breeze, and at the same time the eye of every man who prayed that stronger tradewinds would reveal even more bare suntanned leg. Andrew had insisted that Christine dress somberly, but obviously had not been able to control his daughter's wardrobe choices, Christine noted.

She also noted that Jenny was less flirtatious than usual. This opportunity to show herself off in front of a cadre of attractive uniformed men would on previous days have brought out her most obvious posturings and giggles. But today she seemed quite content to hover near Nick's elbow, staring up at him, affecting total absorption as he explained to her something they'd just been shown on their tour below decks.

The Squadron Commander rose to make a speech extolling the performance of the destroyer on its recent missions. It was designed to act in an anti-submarine warfare role, prepared for shore bombardments, surface warfare actions, anti-aircraft warfare, and landings of helicopters. Christine gave a sad shake of her head as she thought of the poor defenseless little fishing boat Nick had told her about, and she glanced over to him to see if he was thinking likewise, but a pious expression of seriousness obscured any of his real thoughts.

A plaque had been made up, decorated with the ship's coat of arms, and one was given to the man leaving the command, and one was also given to Christine. She stood up to accept it, completely at ease in her role despite having so many eyes upon her. After another rousing band number, the ceremonies were over and everyone was milling about on the deck, shaking hands.

Christine watched with some amount of envy as Nick drew Jenny aside, and they leaned against a bulkhead out of the wind to chat and laugh together. That's what Christine missed most of all in her life: someone with whom she could share all the humor, pathos, drama, and tedium of daily life. Someone to talk to.

"You seem awfully quiet today, Christine," Andrew said, coming up to join her.

"Yes, I guess I am," Christine responded, and then could not think of another thing to say.

"I think I'd better take Mother home. This outing has tired her," Andrew said after a silent moment. He urged his mother with a flick of his wrist to come and join their conversation, and the woman who had been standing apart staring sullenly away from Christine finally walked over to join them.

Christine found herself reaching out to shake hands with the woman who had served for the past few years as the mother figure in her life. Mrs. Hanover neither came close enough for a hug, nor responded warmly enough for a kiss on the cheek to seem welcome.

"Mrs. Hanover, I'm sorry to hear that you want to hurry home already. It's such a beautiful day, I thought maybe you'd take a walk with me around the harbor area."

"Now that my life is so inactive, the least little thing seems to exhaust me," she moaned, and Christine felt a guilty twinge as she saw how the woman had been aged already by her self-pity over Christine's supposed desertion.

"Now, Mrs. Hanover. You still have Andrew, and of course Jenny, to keep you busy," Christine said, refusing to accept all the blame for the woman's isolation.

"Did I hear my name mentioned?" Jenny asked, joining them with Nick in tow.

Her father said sternly, "I think you'd better come with me now, Jenny. I'm going to take your Grandmother home, and you have a party tonight to dress for."

"Oh, no, Daddy. Nick wants to take the boat trip out to the *Arizona* Memorial. I promised I'd go with him."

Christine was surprised to notice Andrew's moment of hesitation. It had been his idea to throw his daughter to the writer, hoping she would win him over, and obviously his plan was working. But perhaps it was working too well, and he was having doubts about his impressionable young daughter arousing too much of Nick's virile interest. But he never won any confrontations with his daughter, and after extracting her promise to be home by five, he left her with Nick to go drive his mother home.

Jenny and Nick rushed off together, forgetting all about Christine. She watched them start to leave the ship, and rather than melting into the crowd and letting them off easy, she followed right behind them down the steps to the dock. Some unreasoned drive within her told her not to fall to the mat and throw the fight just yet.

When Nick and Jenny turned around and noticed her behind them all alone, politeness forced Nick to say, "Would you like to go with us over to the Halawa Landing and take the Pearl Harbor tour?"

She said, "Why, yes, I'd like to. I've never been on that," and she ignored Jenny's spiteful stare at her intrusion, which would create an awkward threesome.

They waited with the other tourists lined up at the Visitors Center, Christine with a serene smile upon her face, Jenny blustering and bragging about the many dates and appointments she'd shared with Nick in recent days, and Nick ignoring them both to study the battle displays.

When they boarded the tiny open vessel that would take them across the harbor to the white concrete and steel structure that had been built to span the 186-foot hull of the sunken *U.S.S. Arizona*, Jenny cleverly arranged the seating so that she was beside Nick, and Christine, odd man out, was seated across from them, between a man wearing three cameras and a woman chewing gum.

The boat bobbed through the water, and the voice of the Petty Officer came over the PA telling them what they would see at the memorial, but Christine was oblivious to it all. After one quick glance back toward Sea Landing, where they were pulling away from David's ship, the *Brewster*, she turned back to watch Nick and Jenny with a detached sort of amusement.

I'm all dressed up like the sorrowing widow again, but I'm no longer a part of it. It's over at last. I've moved away from all those stifling entanglements just as surely as we're moving away from that dock. And I will not go back to that old way again, ever. I won't because I know now that I'm alive, and I love it!

The reason she knew she was alive was that it had suddenly hit her that she was jealous of Jenny. She hated the girl for sitting so possessively hunched up against Nick, for leaning too close to catch his every comment, for touching his knee with such knowing confidence.

I'm not just alive, I'm more than alive. I'm in love!

The feeling was so delicious that she felt as if she were wearing a special glow the people around her could see. In fact, Nick and Jenny had stopped reacting to each other and were both staring at Christine, obviously mystified by her stupidly satisfied smile.

It felt good to be jealous, just as it had felt good the other night to be angry at Nick, when she had screamed at him to get out of her apartment. All the passion of jealousy and anger was infinitely better than the years of hollow passivity she'd pretended when she was living under the Hanover roof, going about her life on that sterile schedule, trying to please everyone but herself.

She was the first one to leap up out of her seat and

disembark at the memorial, and she walked about, talking with total strangers as she told them how amazingly Pearl Harbor had survived the Japanese bombing of December 7, 1941, in which the *Arizona* and its crew had been lost. She recounted how reconstruction had begun at once, and the Navy base here had come back to function as a Pacific base of naval operations throughout the war. Wasn't it all heroic, wasn't it all a triumph of human survival?

When she tried to describe for Nick the importance of Pearl Harbor to the defense of the Pacific today, as they watched the flag being brought down from the flagpole that was attached to the mast of the rusting relic they could see outlined in the water beneath them, he gave her an amused smile.

"You don't have to sell me; I'm already a believer. I'm going to do my next book on the importance of strengthening the Pacific fleet."

They got on the next boat back to shore, and then Christine remembered that Jenny had a date for the evening, apparently some party with her super-active young beach friends that Nick was not going to attend, and an impish plot came to her mind. She was so brimming over with love that she didn't care what Jenny thought, or what Jenny might tattle to her father. She had to see Nick alone just once more. She wanted to find out if her jealousy was well founded, if he truly cared for Jenny. She wanted to know just how hopeless was her newly realized love for the writer. Was there any chance of a future with him or was that impossible? She'd already been given back the gift of life: could she dare to expect it to be a life with perfect love in it?

"Have fun at your party tonight, Jenny," she said. And before the girl could think up some smart remark with which to deflect her, she continued. "Since you're left on your own tonight, Nick, would you like to come by my place and have dinner with me?"

The look he gave her was almost as filled with suspicion as it was with surprise. She decided she'd better confirm her plan quickly, before he decided she was up to something.

"Say about seven o'clock? Oh, we're going right past the submarine base. There's the *Hawkbill* and the *Swordfish*. And there's the diving tower. You know, Jenny, it's filled with water, and they put men in at the bottom and they have to swim up to the top, fifty feet, before they complete submarine school. Isn't that something!"

CHAPTER EIGHT

ON HER WAY HOME, Christine stopped off at the gigantic Pearlridge shopping center. The complex of stores and shops was so large that a monorail ran between the rooftop of the first mall and the third level of the second mall. She knew what she was looking for, so went straight to the Japanese department store, Dai'ei. In the housewares section upstairs she found what she wanted: a wok. Back downstairs again she browsed through the Japanese bakery and the fresh fish displays, and picked up some essential ingredients for the Oriental cooking she was going to try tonight.

Before getting into her car she looked down from the parking lot onto the swampy watercress fields of the Sumida Farm, an odd anachronistic leftover from a less urban time in Hawaii. She saw the pickers in rubber boots and water-proof aprons walking carefully on the tiles dividing the family farm that had somehow escaped the real estate de-velopers.

She decided she'd stop at a supermarket next and get some of this mild local watercress and some crisp Manoa lettuce for a salad. And for dessert, she'd flame some island mangoes as a subtle reminder for Nick of the day they first met and got to know each other over a tray of fruit in his suite at the hotel.

When she got home there was barely time to freshen up her lipstick and tighten a few stray hairpins, for she had to study the wok cookbook and prepare the fresh vegetables and chicken she intended to stir-fry in her gleaming new pan.

She had just set the table when Nick arrived, and she ushered him out to the lanai while she went to the kitchen to mix rum into the Mai Tai mix she'd bought for their drinks. She decorated both glasses with spears of pineapple and maraschino cherries and brought them out with her as she went to join him in admiring the darkening view.

Nick took a long thirsty swallow of his drink, then stopped suddenly. "I'm not sure I should be enjoying this so much. After all, I'm in the home of an alcoholism crusader."

"Oh, please," she said taking a sip. "Total abstinence is necessary for some, but since we don't have any problem, let's enjoy ourselves."

"Fine by me. You're the expert."

"Not an expert quite yet. But I'm working on it. You know, Kim has already told me she wants me to take a management skills class at the University of Hawaii next semester. And she thinks that some day I could become a teacher of facilitator-trainees."

"You're really dedicated to this work, aren't you?"

"I've learned that alcohol abusers can be stopped before they become addicted. And they must be. My mother was killed in an automobile accident after she'd had too much to drink. She was so despondent after my father died, and I didn't know how to help her."

"I'm sorry, that must have been a bad time for you," he said, obviously moved by her confession of the unhappiest part of her past.

Nick seemed to be thinking about her, staring out toward the accordion-pleated mountains of the Koolau Range. It was still light enough to pick out the pattern of the light green kukui trees against the darker green foliage behind them. The encroaching night seemed peaceful, carrying with it a promise of hours of further personal revelations by both of them, of unhurried congeniality, and growing appreciation of each other that just might find its way to the physical expression she craved from him. She sighed to release the pent-up urge to be in his arms, and slipped out of her shoes and curled her legs up under her on the chair.

Nick was saying, "You take great pride in your work, don't you?"

"Yes, my boys are very important to me. Each one who comes into the office is a new challenge. I want to tell him how valuable and precious are the days he's been given, and how much there is to enjoy, if he'll stay sober."

"I'll bet every one of them falls in love with you," he said quietly, studying her animated face.

"That would only be natural. It's easy to fall in love with the person who saves us."

Before she could go on and tell him, specifically, how that had happened to her, he abruptly changed the subject.

"So, you've got the perfect combination. You love your work and you get to do it here in this paradise world you're lucky enough to live in. How did you ever happen to come here to the islands in the first place, Christine?"

"Well, my mother was killed so soon after my father died that I guess I was in shock. On impulse, I decided to take what little money they had left me and blow it all on one big trip, and try to forget all the unhappiness."

"You must have liked it here, because you've never left."

"Well, things happened very quickly. I met David almost the first night I ventured out of my hotel. And the next thing I knew I was the wife of a local citizen and after that I just took the place for granted. In the four years I've lived here, I never thought much about how much I loved the place, or why I did. Not until recently, when I've started looking around me." She put her drink down on the small rattan table between them to lean forward and look into his observant eyes. "You've helped me appreciate the aloha atmosphere, Nick. It's not just poi and ukeleles. It's the friendly people and the good times."

"But your loving bridegroom never bothered to introduce you to the place that was to be your new home."

She leaned back in her chair, the moment having passed

when she could go further, tell him what he had come to mean to her happiness.

"He was busy, he didn't realize..."

"He was selfish! Can't you admit the man had a tiny flaw or two?"

"Of course I can, now."

"Here the man had an eager and vibrant pupil, just waiting to be taught all the wonders of life, and he ignored her needs completely." Nick turned his gaze upon her. "He killed off your spirit, and I can't forgive him for that," he said, his eyes ablaze.

"Well, no permanent damage was done," Christine said lightly, dismissing the subject as quickly as she could.

The spell had been broken, and rather than linger on the subject that always sparked controversy between them, she excused herself to go to the kitchen and make the final dinner preparations.

Nick followed her almost at once, and he stood in the doorway to her small kitchen, watching her tear lettuce into a salad bowl. He seemed to regret the note of conflict he had introduced in their conversation, and he switched to lighter subjects, for which she was relieved.

"You've turned very domestic, all of a sudden," he observed.

"I haven't had a kitchen to play around in for a long time. It's fun; I enjoy it. Do you want to see my new toy? I bought it today, just for this special occasion. It's a wok."

Nick walked over and picked up the deep metal bowl. "And you're going to experiment on me with your new cooking techniques. Well, I hope I live through this evening. You didn't invite me here to poison me, and be rid of the intrepid reporter and his questions once and for all, did you?"

Christine laughed at his joke, then hoped that the searching look he was giving her had no special meaning behind it.

"Here, take these salad plates to the table, will you?" she asked him. "Maybe the activity will divert that active imagination of yours."

The mood after that was easygoing again, and their conversation so unforced that before the evening was over, Christine was sure she would gain the courage to tell him everything she needed him to know. And if her winning streak kept going, perhaps he would tell her what she wanted to hear. Nick stayed in the kitchen until dinner was ready to serve. When she took their plates to the table, he followed her to the dining alcove at the end of her long living room.

He turned her table radio on to a music station, and the room was filled with candlelight, sweet songs, and the intermingled scents of soy sauce, scallions, and ginger. Christine had never been so happy, serving as hostess in her own home to a man who meant so much to her.

During dinner Nick talked very little, seeming content to let her amuse him with stories of all the places she'd visited and the things she'd seen during these past few weeks of tourism. She was careful to let him know that she'd gone to most of the places alone, but that when an escort was a necessity she had dragged an unenthusiastic Andrew along with her a couple of times.

It was only as they finished dinner and she was clearing away the plates that Christine began to feel a bit uneasy. Nick had told her the last time of his distrust of her motives, and now she wished he would warm up just a bit more to reassure her that those unjustified criticisms of his were now forgotten. His talk so far had been cool and impersonal, and he had made no move to touch her, or to show her any special affection. And Christine's heart was crying out for that solace: that was the reason she had invited him here.

She decided she would just have to keep him interested in the topics she could discuss, keep his brain stimulated and enthralled, until his subconscious mind let go of those old and now useless antagonisms. She decided to bring up a plan to him that she had secretly been nurturing for several weeks.

"I think you should do a book on the subject of the Navy's alcohol and drug rehabilitation work," she said brightly, settling back down at the table.

Nick looked hard at her for a moment before responding.

"I've been trying to figure out why you invited me here. Now I know. You just want to tout a book idea."

"No," she laughed. "That wasn't the reason. But since you're here, tell me what you think of the idea. You could go to San Diego and interview the people there, then to the University of West Florida where our work was first re- searched . . ."

"Go anywhere but Hawaii, is that the plan?"

"Kim would be glad to show you around the operation here, but I meant that you usually like to do in-depth re- search."

"Sometimes too in-depth to suit you, am I right?"

"In this case, I'd like to see you follow up every lead. But most of all, you should interview the NASAP partici- pants."

Nick stood up and left the table and began pacing, circling her living room like a huge animal trapped in a tight circus cage. Christine's enthusiasm for her work propelled her on.

"And wait until you see the statistics. For instance, ac- cidents due to the use of alcohol one year cost the Navy eight and a half million dollars. But our preventative course costs us less than two hundred dollars a man to administer."

"All right, Christine. Enough! If I decide to do a book or an article on the subject I can dig out all the numbers myself."

"I'm sorry. I forget what I'm doing when I start talking about my job."

"I don't think you've forgotten for a moment what you're doing."

He came back to the dining alcove to stand over her, watching her.

Nick's enigmatic words broke the spell that had caused her to run off on this tangent. The idea of working with Nick on a book on her favorite topic had been an appealing one, and she hoped she hadn't killed the idea for him with her bombardment of material.

She jumped up nervously. "I have to finish clearing off

these dishes." She put her hand on his arm as she asked, "Do you want some coffee?"

"Not now," he said, staring down at her hand, suddenly conspicuous on his sleeve.

Christine stayed in the kitchen as long as she could, needing time to reconnoiter. Somehow things were going badly. It was as though she and Nick were out of sync, not thinking along the same lines as she'd hoped they might. He had seemed interested in her work, but then had become coldly aloof about becoming involved in it.

Perhaps all the time he had spent with Jenny had changed him. Where once he had worked overtime at pleasing Christine, now his mind seemed to be with someone else. He no longer wanted Christine's input for his book on David Hanover. He had the awed and eager-to-please Jenny at his beck and call now. And she was young, nubile, and full of fun. Apparently it was going to be hard to win back his interest. In fact, it just might be too late, she considered sadly, stacking plates in an untidy tilting heap.

When Christine went back to join Nick she found him sitting in the living room. He was wearing a barong shirt from the Philippines made of fine white cotton with intricate white embroidery that made him seem exotic and somewhat out of reach. Sitting outside the circle of light from her one lamp, he seemed inscrutable, his wavy dark hair shading the upper part of his face so that the mellowness of his eyes was hidden.

Earlier, when he had arrived, he'd been carrying a wrapped package that he put down on the couch. Now he reached over and tossed it across to her as she came into the room.

"Here, I brought this hostess gift for you."

Truly pleased, she said, "How nice of you."

"I didn't know what your motives were for inviting me here this evening, so I thought I'd behave like a welcome guest."

"Which of course you are," she smiled, coming to sit beside him as she unwrapped the small box. Inside was a bottle of expensive Hawaiian perfume.

"If you hold it up to the light, you'll see that there's a real orchid inside the bottle," he said.

She held the bottle up and tilted it from side to side so that the tiny purple flower floated about like a lifeboat.

"Aren't you going to open it and see if you like it?" he asked.

The perfume was a penetrating essence of orchid and plumeria and pikake, all the earthy smells of the land she had so recently learned to love. She dabbed some on her neck, just behind her ears, and it was just like putting on a lei of fresh flowers.

Nick had closed his eyes in a dreamy appreciation of the perfume, and Christine was happy to see that something had brought a look of pleasure to his face. She made use of the opportunity to watch him unobserved for a moment. She studied the lacy mat of eyelashes pulled down over his eyes, closing her out, and the deep laugh lines around his mouth, and she imagined that this was what he looked like as he slept, especially when he was in the throes of a satisfying erotic dream.

"Lovely," he said. "That stuff smells better on you than it did in the store."

"I'll sit nice and close so you can appreciate it," she said, scrunching over to sit closer to him. "I think it does a lot to improve my image, don't you?" she said, smoothing the prim dress she was still wearing from this afternoon's ceremonies.

"I'm not fooled. Perfume or not, I don't think you've changed at all."

"You don't?"

"I watched you today at that ship, playing your old role. You were completely happy and comfortable."

"Yes, but I never used to be, don't you see? I can do that now when I'm called upon and not mind it. There's no more phoniness to it because it doesn't dominate my entire life."

"I think you're still paying service to the past, wearing your hair all tightly coiled, and those ridiculous shapeless uniforms of yours. Can't you get out of those widow's

weeds?" he said, meaning it figuratively, but his words gave
Christine an idea.

"I'll go change my clothes," she said. "I didn't have time
earlier." She knew that this somber style of dress had always
offended him. Perhaps if she put on one of her gay new
prints he would be cheered by it. She stood up and started
for the bedroom.

"You're just going to go 'slip into something more comfortable.' That's the line the Mata Haris always use. And
then they come out in some terribly sexy piece of net that
is obviously very uncomfortable."

She turned to look at him, a worried reaction wrinkling
her brow in spite of the happy atmosphere she had pledged
herself to maintain this evening.

"I was just going to put on my new holomuu, the one
you liked so much. I thought that would please you."

He stood up and came toward her slowly. "And it seems
to be very important that you please me this evening." His
eyes seemed stormy, as if an unexpected tide was causing
tempestuous surges in their dark blue depths.

She shrank back in the doorway, some instinct warning
her that she should be afraid of this odd restive quality in
him.

"It will only take me a moment to change," she said
softly.

When he was close enough to touch her he reached out
and slowly ran one hand from her shoulder to her hip,
outlining the curves as he spoke quietly, almost hypnoti-
cally.

"Satin would be nice, sensuous satin in a gleaming cream
color, with maribou feathers at the neckline, showing just
a peek now and then of the bulging breasts beneath."

His hand roved over the bodice of her loose twill, teasing
with the touch. The stimulating effect of his hands upon
her was not diminished by his seeming sarcasm. She leaned
back and closed her eyes, made faint by the onrush of desire
that was taking control of her senses. The sound of his voice
alone, no matter what the words he was intoning, could
have put her in this receptive state. But his searching hands,

giving her body shape as they pressed impudently against the thin fabric of the dress, sent her mind reeling. She felt her knees weaken beneath her, and she sagged back from him in even more of a stupor, not strong enough to initiate a move away from him.

"Or black lace might be even better," he purred, taking her shoulders in both hands and pulling her toward him so that she fell against his broad chest with almost-hypnotized limpness, like a magician's assistant, made ready for the sawing-in-half trick.

"You little vixen. You're trying to seduce me, aren't you?" he said, his fingers suddenly tightening their grip as his sharp words hissed against her ear.

"Of course not. How can you think such a thing?" she demanded as she awakened quickly from her foggy dream-like state.

"You invited me here to make one last attempt to lead the pack of hunters away from their helpless victim. This new idea you've thought up to involve me in...you're trying to draw me into another project, get me away from the book you're so afraid of. The book that would reveal the truth about your marriage to that worthless scoundrel."

The blues and greens raging about in his deep eyes were like a cold wave breaking over her, and she pulled loose from him with invigorated strength. She ran to her bedroom, and had just crossed to her bed when she realized that he had followed her. As she turned around to confront him, he gave one brutal lunge and pushed her, sprawling, back across her bed.

"You're playing with fire, little girl," he said savagely, throwing himself on one knee beside her. "You've known how hard it has been for me to keep my hands off of you. I've wanted you from that first moment I saw you. Now you're trying a dangerous game, one you know nothing about. And you're liable to get hurt."

He looked down into her pleading eyes with no sympathy, then slowly, menacingly let the full weight of his body fall on top of her. The breath was forced out of her lungs by the impact of his weight pressing her into the mattress. But her fitful gasp for air was stopped by his mouth pressed ruthlessly upon hers.

Her mind removed her from the threatening situation by throwing her into a protective fantasy. Before her eyes flashed the image he'd just portrayed for her. She was a seductive temptress, all decked out in plunging necklines and filmy peekaboo transparent net, and she'd been caught at her treachery by this unforgiving villain.

She tried to kick her feet and bounce him away from her, but the effect of all that movement was just more provocative; her struggle caused him to press his lips against hers with even more cruelty than before.

Then her mental picture suddenly switched to a woman in love, kissing the man she loved, receiving loving gestures she wanted to return, and she reached up to put her hands around Nick's neck, pressing her fingers lovingly into the uncut fringe of dark hair that poured over his collar so abundantly.

NIck gave a shuddering response to the touch of her fingers and pushed himself up on one elbow to look into her eyes.

"I'm not made of stone, you know. I'm a real flesh-and-blood man. I don't think you know what you're doing to me."

He bent to kiss her throat, right where the pulsing warmth of the passion coursing through her gave her away.

"I'm only showing you what I feel. It's wrong to bury what's in your heart; you showed me that."

She watched with disappointment as the fire in his eyes burned down to a cold blue flame of cynicism.

"I know exactly what you feel. It's the official Hanover family pact. Throw the intruder off guard. Distract him from his mission."

"Oh, Nick, no. You don't understand . . ."

"You've done your work too well to stop now, Chris," he said with a husky sigh.

He grabbed her by the shoulders, pulling her roughly toward him as he rolled off of her and onto his back. Her dress pulled against her and as she twisted in his grasp she felt the buttons down the front of her bodice begin to strain. Then the tug of his hands intensified as he clutched her to him and she felt small popping explosions as one by one' the buttons began to release and her dress tore open down to her waist. Nick felt the hated dress give in to him and pulled harder, ripping the entire thing off of her and throwing it back away from her with a victorious gasp of triumph.

Then he pulled her bare shoulders down to him, so that she was balanced atop him, feeling with her sensitive skin the surges of his chest beneath the white sheeting of his shirt. Now he kissed her with a mouth that throbbed his passionate message of desire to her unmistakably. And her own body's automatic responses almost pirated her aboard the same voyage to oblivion that he was embarked upon. But suddenly, mutinously, she pulled away from him with a show of strength that surprised her, and he let go of her as if he'd had cold water splashed in his face. She sat beside him on the bed and, feeling a sob rise up in her throat, pressed one hand to her mouth to silence the frightened sound she was about to make.

She didn't want him to make love to her this way. She had thought he might care for her; she had clung to one last shred of hope that there was something more behind his purely physical desire for her. But there was nothing. Only mistrust and lack of understanding, and raw unfeeling passion.

"Let's call this whole thing off, shall we?" he said coldly. "I can't make love to a manipulating schemer. No matter how she throws her sexiness at me."

He reached down to pick up the brown wad of fabric off the floor, rolled it into a compact ball, and threw it across the room.

Without emotion he stared at Christine, huddled in only her skimpy patches of underwear.

"I could have guessed that underneath that very proper dress you'd be wearing bright red lacy things like that." His lip curled contemptuously. "You've been repressing a flaming sexuality, haven't you?" He laughed with a hollow sound.

If only she could tell him that he was the only one capable

of bringing out these feelings of desire in her. He was the hot match that set her aflame with love, with cravings for the taste, touch, and sight of him, in spite of her efforts to forget him, to learn to survive without him.

"After you've put on something decent, come out where I can talk to you," he said suddenly, getting up and walking out of the room, running a shaking hand through his hair as if to try to calm himself.

She wrapped herself in the kimono and came into the living room to find him sipping another Mai Tai he'd fixed for himself, looking at her as though she were a stranger.

"Do you want me to make that coffee now?" she asked hesitantly, with a dismal feeling of prescience that told her their happy moments together were forever over. "The last time you left without your coffee."

"Forget it. Save the special hospitality for the grateful and devoted Andrew. I want to tell you something. Sit down and quit looking at me like that."

She wasn't aware that she was begging him with her eyes. She only knew that she wanted to cry out for his understanding.

"I want you to know that I'm leaving Hawaii. But before you run over to the Hanover house to take your bows, I also want you to know that it's not because you've convinced me. It wasn't your appeal to help you protect the sensitive feelings of the Hanovers, nor your attempt to deflect me into another book project, and it definitely is not because you've aroused such a passion for you within me that I can deny you nothing. I'm leaving for my own reasons."

"Where are you going?" she asked numbly.

"I'm going back to New York, where I can work and write in peace, without your damnable influence to do otherwise."

"When will you leave?"

"Probably tomorrow, if I can make the reservations that quickly." He clinked the ice in his glass, round and round. "Actually, it was Jenny who gave me the idea. She pointed out this evening when I took her back to her place that I have almost all the interviews I need. The ones that are left to do wouldn't be of any value, anyway. You and Andrew and Mrs. Hanover won't give me anything but glorifications."

"Jenny's been quite a help to you, then."

"She's a very street-wise young lady. She's practical. She convinced me that any more time spent here would be wasted. And tonight has convinced me that any more time spent here could be very distracting."

So, Jenny, after all, had been able to convince him to leave the islands, and once he was away from here he just might decide to abandon the book. Christine had underestimated her young niece. She obviously had powers of persuasion that were not obvious to another woman. But they were tricks that a man like Nick Carruthers would enjoy having worked upon him. Jenny had probably buttered up his ego, entertained him, and kept his mind off anything serious, so that he was in just the right mood to accept her bidding.

"Yes, Jenny has the right idea," he went on, not knowing how his words were hurting the woman who loved him, who sat watching him with hungry eyes. "She says that in New York I will be able to look at the material more objectively, get the right perspective on it."

And, of course, Jenny might soon be returning to her mother on the eastern mainland. She would be close by if Nick needed to summon a sympathetic listener. She would be there, and Christine would be here. Christine couldn't help but wonder if that thought had occurred to the girl.

She took a deep breath. "I think Andrew would want to know. Is Jenny important to you?" she asked, more for herself than her brother-in-law. She had to know what had caused tonight's missed connections.

"Tell him I'm doing this for her, leaving Hawaii. That will make him very happy," he said.

Christine stood up, anxious to show Nick to the door now and close it behind him. She had terrible work to begin. There were days and weeks ahead of her during which she would have to take strong measures to eliminate her preoccupation with Nick. It would take an act of will she wasn't sure she was capable of, but she would square her shoulders and wade into it. She had faced this kind of loss before; at least she was experienced.

Each time she had handled the situation differently. After the loss of her parents, when she was still resilient and spontaneous, she had splurged everything on a vacation. After the loss of her husband she had turned for security to his family. But now, with the loss of Nick, she planned to throw herself into her work and her new life as an active young woman. She planned to put her faith only in herself this time.

Nick followed her almost reluctantly to the door, as if there was something else on his mind. He started to speak, then stopped, cleared his throat, and began again.

"I'm worried about you, Christine. I'm afraid that the Hanovers still have a hold on you, that you'll drift right back into your old patterns of life with them."

"There's no reason for you to worry about deserting me amongst the enemy. I'm strong; I'll stick it out," she said with a pale smile.

"You won't give up this apartment and move back to them, will you?"

"No, I won't."

"And you won't let them talk you into a marriage to Andrew, unless that's what you really want?"

"No, I won't." The idea was so outrageous that she almost laughed in his face. How could she ever love any man but Nick? And she certainly would never fall in love with her spiritless brother-in-law, no matter how lonely the days ahead.

He was standing close to her now, at the door. He reached up and pulled a hairpin out of her bedraggled hairdo, and threw it over his shoulder.

"And promise me you'll let your hair down, and leave it down. Even for Navy balls." He withdrew another pin and tossed it over his other shoulder. "And Change of Command ceremonies." Another pin flew behind him. "And lunch dates with Mrs. Hanover." As the last pin was sent across the room her hair came cascading down around her shoulders in a burst of freedom. He fluffed it with both of his hands, then bent down with an almost affectionate move to kiss it lightly where he held it bunched in one hand.

Christine clenched her fists, trying to resist the temptation to put her arms around him, for he had not moved, but was frozen in position, bent with his face in her hair.

"That damned perfume," he muttered as he straightened up. "What was I saying? Oh, yes, promise me that you'll keep your freedom. Cherish it, and don't let anyone take it away from you again."

"I promise," she said, looking up into his eyes and wondering why this was so important to him when she herself was not. Then she remembered with a sigh of resignation just why she loved him so much. He was a man who automatically fought for the underdog. And he fought rough and hard for them. His books had shown her that. He had reacted to the plight he'd found her in with instant empathy. Freeing her from the control of David's family had become a crusade for him, and he did not want to fail in it.

"I've made my break with the past," she said to reassure him. "I don't plan to crawl back into my shell. So save your pity for the downtrodden of the world. I will be fine."

She couldn't stand to think that he would be flitting about on exciting assignments, meeting Jenny for a rendezvous in Manhattan now and then, escorting beautiful sophisticated women around the capital cities of the world, and meanwhile feeling a twinge of pity now and then for the pathetic Navy widow on Oahu he hadn't been able to save. She was too proud to let that happen.

"I have my new clothes, my new apartment, my new job, and lots of tourism to do. What could be better? My life is complete."

Achingly, she thought of what was missing. There was going to be a gap in her life where love was supposed to be. And that gap would grow if she wasn't careful. She'd have to work very hard at walking around it, looking away from it, ignoring it.

He started for the door. "Goodbye, Christine."

"I'm sorry," she called to stop him.

"What?" Standing in the dark hall, he already seemed unreachable to her.

"I'm sorry that tonight was such a disaster," she said.

"It was inevitable," he said, turning to start the long walk down the hall, his shoulders more slumped than usual.

"Thanks for the perfume, at least," she said.

"Thanks for the dinner, at least," he said, his voice turning the corner with him.

"I wish you had let me explain," she called softly.

But he was gone. "I wasn't trying to lure you away from your work tonight." She was talking to empty darkness. "I only wanted to tell you that I love you," she whispered into the void.

CHAPTER NINE

IT HAD BECOME a habit to spend Sunday night at the Malones. If Peter was in town, he often invited some young fellow officer to join them, and they had a foursome. But Christine had grown tired of this obvious matchmaking, which she knew was intended to cheer her up, and tonight she· was relieved that Peter was on duty and she and Kim were eating alone together, on trays in the living room of Kim's naval housing unit.

"Well, I'm happy at last to have heard the whole story," Kim said as she carried in a pot of tea.

"It's been too painful to discuss until now, Kim, or I would have confided in you long before this."

"I didn't press you because I had suspected most of it already. One look at your face that day when Nick walked into the P.C.T. and I knew I was looking at love. You were so funny, denying it."

"I didn't know, myself, at that point," she sighed.

"I think the whole world knows about it now. You've moped around these past few weeks like one of the walking wounded. Even those wild Hawaiian prints you've been wearing don't do much to help."

"I hope my dismal attitude hasn't affected my work," Christine said.

"No, of course not. You're too good at what you do to let that happen. Tea?"

"Yes, please," Christine said, pulling up a pillow to sit in front of the low coffee table where their red lacquer trays were resting.

"And I'm very relieved that I've been able to count on your help at the office, Christine, because I'm going to lean on you more in the months ahead. I may even want you to fill in for me on one of those mainland trips that's coming up."

"I'm pleased that you're showing such faith in me. But I don't think I'm ready for..."

"Don't you want to go to Florida for a weekend?"

"Yes, but why don't you want to go?"

"My doctor has advised me to take it easy for a while."

"Oh, Kim, what's wrong?"

"Nothing's wrong. It's just that Peter and I finally got together on the right night at the right time and now I'm going to get that big *opu* my mama wanted."

"That's wonderful! I'm so excited for you."

Her friend's obvious happiness relieved some of the pain in her own heart, for she knew how much the Malones wanted children. Then she was reminded of the golden dreams she had spun not too long ago. A baby by Nick! How happy and complete she would feel right now if she were carrying one, right next to her heart.

She got up and went to Kim, understanding how blessed she must feel, and gave the girl's slim shoulders a quick hug.

"I'll be available to do whatever you need. You just sit with your feet up and give me my orders."

"Can you go to a five-day-a-week schedule, right away?" Kim asked, taking advantage of Christine's offer.

Christine thought about it just for a moment.

"That's just what I need, as a matter of fact. With more working hours I'll have less free time to walk the beach and kick at the sand."

"And think about the man that got away?"

"Yes," Christine said sadly.

They both began to eat, then Christine remembered something.

"Oh, except next Friday. I almost forgot that appointment with Andrew. His secretary called me today and said he had to see me in his office. It must be something important."

"Like ordering your new checks," Kim said irreverently.

They both laughed uproariously at the thought of the officious Andrew, making much ado about nothing, as usual.

Christine felt fortunate indeed to have a good friend like Kim to share joys and sorrows with. Tonight, before hearing Kim's wonderful news, Christine had given her friend a blow-by-blow account of her short but life-altering acquaintance with Nick Carruthers. As she leaned against the sink watching Kim expertly stir a sweet and sour sauce that brought a pucker of hunger to the inside of her mouth, she felt the balm of her friend's attentive listening and knew that with friends like this to count on, she would be all right.

The past weeks had been frustrating for Christine. She explained it to Kim as feeling like a jet plane, revving up its engines noisily at the start of the runway, but with nowhere to go. If Nick had remained in her life she would have had someone with whom to share all this exhilaration. She would have had a direction for the new energies that flowed through her. Now she had her new life of independence, and she was enjoying it to the fullest, but it lacked the comforting foundation of Nick's presence to make it perfect.

She shrugged her shoulders as she began to eat dinner with Kim, thinking that perhaps she was asking too much of life to expect perfection. Looking across at the glow on Kim's cheeks she envied her friend who had it all—an adoring husband, the beginnings of a family, a stimulating job she was good at, and a joy for life that was either the result, or the cause, of all that good fortune.

Friday was always Aloha Day in Honolulu, and it was observed even in the financial district where Andrew had his office. Christine noticed that all the secretaries who worked in the Financial Plaza on Bishop Street were hurrying past her in flowered muu-muus and skimpy sandals.

How incongruous it seemed to see these long-haired beauties settle down behind typewriters and tellers' windows attired in dresses as bright as the plumage of jungle birds. Christine gave an appreciative smile, enjoying the uniqueness of this strange land that Nick had taught her to appreciate.

Andrew was on his feet waiting at his office door to greet Christine as she came down the hall past the secretarial pool.

"I was hoping you'd be on time, my dear. Today is such a busy day."

"I apologize for not being early, as I always used to be," she said so softly as she walked past him into the office that he missed the joke.

"You are wearing that Hawaiian perfume again," Andrew sniffed, turning to follow her close at the heels, as if enchanted by the very stuff he was critical of. "I noticed it the other night, but I assumed you only doused yourself in it when you were going out for social occasions."

"Don't worry, your cigarette smoke will soon blot out any of the sweet garden smells I may have brought in here with me."

Andrew had dropped into a huge leather chair behind his desk to grab a cigarette he was about to light.

"Sorry, does this bother you?" he asked with a nervous glance her way. He seemed uneasy around her lately, incapable of understanding her new moods and wary of her attempts to take control of their relationship and lighten it with her gentle teasing. He was at once embarrassed and captivated by her recent aggressiveness in inviting him to accompany her on excursions into the Hawaiian nightlife, where she would try to get him to loosen his stiff tie and relax and enjoy himself.

"I'm used to your smoking; go ahead," Christine waved her okay to him and sat down. "Now, what is this important matter we have to discuss here in your office?"

"It's Nick Carruthers we have to talk about, Christine."

She involuntarily crossed her arms at chest level and then locked them in place, as if to protect herself from the onslaught of bright white emotions his mere name evoked.

"What about him?" she asked, trying to appear casual.

"You see this file? These are copies of letters I've sent to him in the past few weeks. None has been answered. Not a word from him since his abrupt departure. I think he's lost interest in our project. Something has gone wrong, Christine."

He said the last few words with such a narrow-eyed hostility that she felt he was trying to make her feel personally responsible for the unreliable writer's actions.

"Jenny tells me you had dinner with him the night before he suddenly vanished from our midst. Can you recall anything from that evening that would shed some light on our little mystery?"

She could recall every nuance, every glimmer, every word that had been exchanged that fateful night; she had reviewed them in her head so many times.

"No, I'm afraid not," she said turning to look out the office window.

"But it was your responsibility to keep track of him, to keep the family aware of what he was doing."

"You pulled me off that assignment, don't you remember? Jenny told me you wanted her to be in charge of influencing Mr. Carruthers."

"Why, I never said any such thing. I didn't like it one bit when she began spending time with him and I told her so. But she said someone had to work with him. And since you were acting so bizarre, moving out of Mother's house and behaving as though you wanted nothing more to do with the Hanovers, she convinced me we shouldn't count on you for any more assistance," he said glumly, showing his suspicion that his daughter might have outwitted him again some way.

Christine had to consider with amazement the young girl's talent for mischief. Now it was clear that Jenny had blatantly lied to Christine, and like a naive fool, she had never suspected it. The girl must have wanted the wealthy and famous writer all to herself, and to further that campaign she had decided to remove Christine from the competition. She had even been canny enough to count on the sagging lines of communication between Christine and the Hanovers at that time to keep her lie unrevealed.

The irony of the situation was that although Jenny probably didn't care a bit one way or another about the planned book, she had said she would distract Nick from the project, and she had somehow done it. Why had she convinced him to suspend his work here and leave? But of course! She'd sent Nick back to the mainland just at the time when Christine began giving her some trouble—in fact, on the very day that Christine started to prop up her end of the triangle again by inviting Nick to dinner.

"Is Jenny going to return to her mother any time soon?" Christine asked. She knew the question would make no sense to Andrew, since it existed only in context with her own need to discern the girl's motives.

"She's talked abut it, yes; I hope to get her safely back to her mother's care soon. I'm much too old to begin this kind of fatherly responsibility. Now, let's get back to the subject. Why do you think the man is ignoring my letters? Do you think he is going to drop the book idea?"

"Oh, Andrew. I wish that was true."

"What do you mean? We want this story told."

"I have hesitated to worry you about this until now, Andrew, because I thought you wanted me to stay out of it. That's what Jenny told me, and I believed her."

"You should have known better. Well, go on."

"I've come to the conclusion that Mr. Carruthers might write a book that you and your mother will resent terribly. I think he plans to take a very critical look at David's military career."

"Oh, no. You can't be serious." Andrew's face had turned as pale as his hair. "But we brought the idea to him; we suggested the project. Surely he wouldn't take an attitude toward the material we might disapprove of."

"He doesn't care about your disapproval one bit."

"But how could he find anything scurrilous to publish about our dear boy?"

Christine hesitated. "Your brother was only human, Andrew. He made mistakes just like all the rest of us. Since

his death we've forgotten that; we've idealized him. But
Mr. Carruthers is such a thorough researcher that he'll find
out about those mistakes. I think he could find something
shocking in Albert Schweitzer's life story."

"But what makes you think that's what he's going to
do?"

"Because a book of unrelieved praise wouldn't sell. And
this man only wants best sellers. That's how he makes his
living."

"Well, this must be stopped at once. The publisher is a
friend of mine. I'll call John Hicks and have this book
contract canceled."

Andrew began rustling through his telephone book, looking for the listing of the publisher who had become an
acquaintance of his during Hawaiian vacations.

Christine sat watching him with a distracted look, her
thoughts thousands of miles away. She was thinking of the
trip Kim had asked her to take next week to the mainland.
She was to attend NASAP meetings in Florida. She would
be on the east coast in just a few days.

"Someone should go see him," she said. "What if Mr.
Hicks needs persuading?"

Andrew looked up at her, now so agitated that he grabbed
at her idea. "Of course. I'll have to go talk to him in person."

Then he glanced down at his desk calendar and slammed
his fist against his forehead, his ambitious plan of action
quashed. "I can't do that," he moaned. "I have interbank
conferences all week. There's no way I can get to New
York."

"Someone should go," she repeated. An idea was just
beginning to germinate in her mind, one so appealing that
she didn't want to blurt it out too soon; she wanted the idea
to come from Andrew. That way she would know if it was
just some ridiculous flight of fancy.

Andrew was staring at her speculatively. "You'll have
to go in my place. You must finish the project you promised
to undertake for the family."

"Well, I have to go to Pensacola on business next week

for Kim. Perhaps she'd give me one extra day to stop off in New York and see this publisher for you."

He hesitated only an instant while he swallowed any last-minute doubts he may have had about entrusting her with such a delicate assignment in his place. "You must go, Christine. You owe it to the family. It's the least you can do for us, after making such a mess of this Carruthers thing. You should have told me your suspicions about him at once. And you never should have listened to Jenny about anything."

Christine nodded and smiled a cooperative expression in Andrew's direction. Let him think that she was going to agree to this trip because of duty to the family. Let him believe that they could continue forever to use her guilt feelings over her unhappy marriage to David Hanover to get what they wanted from her. Let them go on assuming that she was still the same old Christine inside. It wasn't true.

She wasn't making the effort for the Hanovers at all. She was going to New York, but only because it was convenient with her work schedule, and because she wanted to find out for herself what kind of book the publisher planned. But mostly, she was going to New York because that was where Nick Carruthers lived. Just passing apartment houses where he might live, riding in taxi cabs he might use, and visiting an office he may have been in, would bring his precious memory closer to her, and for that alone the trip would be worth it.

"All right, I'll go," she said, with a fiery anticipation lighting up her eyes and a ring to her voice that had been missing for over three weeks.

Christine had forgotten what life in a busy metropolis was really like. She had been critical of Honolulu for becoming too much a bustling high-rise city, but within a few minutes of entering New York City in a death-defying taxi ride from the airport, she was yearning for the easy tempo and graceful rhythm of life back on her island. She felt conspicuous in her bright hibiscus-yellow suit with the gaily

printed blouse under it, and wondered as she entered the
dingy office building if everyone thought her an unsophis-
ticated island girl.

The publisher's secretary was, however, very friendly
and interested in Christine's long trip. "Mr. Hicks tells me
you live in Hawaii. Lucky you. I hope to go there on vacation someday."

"That's just what I did, only I never left."

"Won't you take a seat? Mr. Hicks is with one of our
writers right now and can't be disturbed."

"A writer you say?" Christine said, cautiously moving
toward a long leather couch in the waiting room. "Anyone
I might know?" she asked, pretending mere idle curiosity.

"I'm sure you'll recognize the name. Nicolas Carruthers.
He's written a good deal about your area of the world."

"Nicolas Carruthers." She tried to achieve the look of
an impressed reader. "Yes, I've read all his books. Say, it's
been a long trip. Could you point out the lady's room? I'd
like to freshen up before I see Mr. Hicks. Do you think
he'll be much longer?"

"It will be only a minute or two. But you have time. Just
go right down that hall to the left."

Christine shot away from the office as if there were wild
tigers about to be let loose from inside. She dawdled in the
rest room, fussing with her new short and breezy haircut,
reapplying her lipstick, and washing her hands several
times. How could she have managed to schedule an appointment immediately after Nick's? Or was this the co-
incidence she had been hoping for without even being aware
of it? When she had formulated this wild idea of coming
to New York, had she planned on just this kind of last
chance to see him? No, she must avoid him, for he would
never sympathize with her reasons for coming to see his
publisher.

She wondered how long she could stay away from the
office to avoid encountering him, without arousing the curiosity of Mr. Hicks. After a few more minutes of pointless
primping she cautiously stepped back into the outside hall
and inched her way back toward Mr. Hicks's office. To her

relief the door to his office was open, indicating his previous caller had left, so she proceeded toward the friendly secretary with more confidence.

"Mr. Hicks will see you now, Mrs. Hanover," the woman said, and Christine started for the office door, happy that her tactic had worked.

"And I will see you after that, Mrs. Hanover," a familiarly husky voice announced next, stopping her in her tracks.

Nick stepped out from the side of a tall bookcase where he had been concealing himself from her view. He was dressed in a dark plaid sports jacket and tan slacks, which made him seem quite different. Whenever she thought about him, she remembered him in light sports shirts, or wrapped in hotel towels. But his immense shoulders seemed no less muscular, his long legs no less strong, and his manner no less dominating for the academic look he had now assumed, complete with leather patches on the elbows of his sleeves and heavy briefcase in one hand.

"How did you know I was here?" she asked, for lack of any great inspiration as to what to say.

Mr. Hicks's secretary piped up. "Just as he was leaving I told him that our next appointment was with a reader of his from Hawaii, then when I told him your name he said he knew you and wanted to surprise you. Isn't it a small world?" she giggled, taking off her reading glasses to stare at them with the curiosity of a hopeless romantic.

Nick lowered his big body onto the leather couch and began tapping one foot impatiently, as if he were going to wait for her if it took all day.

"I know you're anxious to see Mr. Hicks, so I'll wait for you and we'll talk when you come out."

"Oh, all right," she said lightly, wondering how she could endure the next few minutes with a sentence like that hanging over her head. Nick's serious demeanor and unfriendly greeting clearly indicated he felt no special thrill at seeing her. Apparently the secretary had come to the same conclusion, for she put her glasses on again and turned her attention back to the manuscript she was reading, convinced that no interesting sparks were about to fly between the attractive pair in her waiting room.

As Christine walked past the couch she could feel Nick's perusal taking in every inch of her, examining her new hairdo, her bright clothing, and her springy step. She tried to walk tall and proud, full of her new-found confidence, and not let him know how she shuddered at the possibility of any negative comment he might have about her. But he said nothing, just sat watching her walk toward Mr. Hicks's office, his stony stare never leaving her.

It was with great relief that Christine found John Hicks behind his desk and heard him say, "Close the door behind you, will you, Mrs. Hanover? Nice to meet you. I understand you're Andrew Hanover's sister-in-law."

Since she was nervously aware of the confrontation that awaited her outside, Christine took her time establishing her reason for being in his office. She carefully explained Andrew's concerns about what kind of book Mr. Carruthers planned concerning David Hanover, and she chose her words carefully as she described Nick's world-wide notoriety as a writer of controversial material.

"I really don't know what you'e so worried about, Mrs. Hanover," the man behind the desk said, taking off his horn-rimmed glasses to polish them with a large monogrammed handkerchief. "Our Mr. Carruthers is no yellow journalist, grinding out pot boilers just to make a great deal of money. Far from it. He has a very substantial independent income. His parents were both from old textile families, left him a bundle of stocks and bonds. He only takes on a writing project when it seems truly worthwhile to him. And, as a matter of fact, in your case he has decided there isn't enough material there for a book, and the entire project has been scrapped."

"Really?" she gushed in spite of herself. "He's abandoned all plans for a book on my late husband?"

"It sometimes happens—that after the initial research Nick changes his mind. He was just in here, you know, outlining his new plans for a book about the strategic importance of the Pacific fleet. I think it will be quite a sensation, the way he describes it. Yes, it needs to be written, very astute of Nick."

Christine could see that the publisher's mind was already fixed on the new project, so although she wanted to ask more about just why the writer had dropped his previous plan, she decided that, her goal accomplished, she would leave quickly and gracefully. She was gratified that she had been spared the long and unpleasant scene she had foreseen in which she would have to beseech the publisher to pull the rug out from under his writer and cancel the Hanover project. She had pictured herself appealing to his sense of patriotism, begging him to protect her vulnerable family. And she had dreaded every moment of it.

But such dramatics had been unnecessary. Nick had already dropped the book idea, all on his own. She couldn't help wondering what had been the deciding factor. As she shook hands with Hicks and walked out of his office she realized that she would very soon have an opportunity to ask him that herself.

As soon as she opened the office door she saw Nick's familiar huge frame. Just being in New York had changed him into a more intense and highly charged person than he'd been in Hawaii, and that vital energy was expressed in every inch of his tautly held body. He seemed poised ready to spring as he strode toward her. He grabbed her hand and pulled her unceremoniously out of the reception area and down the hall.

"Come on. I haven't another moment to waste. I have a lunch date with my researcher at noon, and I don't want to miss her."

"Thank you, goodbye," Christine called over her shoulder to the startled secretary who watched them disappear down the corridor to the elevators.

Downstairs at the entrance of the building Nick hailed a cab and pushed her into it.

"Where are we going?" she asked.

"To my apartment. It isn't far from here. I want to set a few things straight with you, but I don't plan to miss this appointment on your account."

"Oh, I see," she muttered, knowing that she'd been put in her proper place. Her momentary hopes that he might be whisking her off to some glamorous New York restaurant where the literary types hang out, for an exciting lunch where they would celebrate the conclusion of the work they had briefly shared, were dashed. But at least she was going to his apartment. This trip would leave her with enough memories to warm many a lonely night back home.

His apartment, as she had expected, offered her enough material for months of dreams and speculations.

"Why, this is beautiful," she said as soon as she entered. It was so large and open in feeling that she knew it had to be expensive, and the furnishings, while not extravagant or showy, were obviously of excellent quality. The sofas were covered in real leather, the wooden chests and tables were authentic English antiques, and the carpet was an old Oriental still in perfect condition. But the major decorations in the apartment were books: floor-to-ceiling bookcases lined every available wall, and were filled to overflowing with hardback books, notebooks, stacks of papers, paperback books, and bound manuscripts.

Nick strode over to the large window and flipped open the shutters with a discouraged sigh. "You can see why I was considering moving my home base to Hawaii. How would you like to try to work while gazing at a view like this?"

A skyline of rooftops and spires saluted her from outside the window, inspiring in its own right, but no rival for the palm trees, wide-open green parks, and jewel-green ocean outside most any window in Honolulu.

Nick went into an adjoining room that was apparently his study and workroom to drop his briefcase on his desk. While he was gone, a small Oriental woman came into the living room, startling Christine with her amazing resemblance to Mrs. Wang.

"Oh, good. You here for lunch, now. I have it all ready."

"No, I'm not the one coming for lunch. That is, I think Mr. Carruthers has invited someone else to lunch."

"You stay, too? I set another place."

"That's not necessary, Miko. Mrs. Hanover can only stay for a few moments."

The housekeeper looked surprised at Nick's show of rudeness. She left the room as quietly as she had come in.

"I don't want to interrupt your meeting," Christine said softly, hoping she would at least be here long enough to get a glimpse of this "researcher" he was so anxious to meet for the intimate luncheon for two at home. She was probably young and gorgeous, and given to hanging over his shoulder when he was at the typewriter, eager to be of any help she could.

"I want to know what you're doing in New York, Christine. In particular, what you were doing in the office of my publisher," he said, getting down to the subject at hand.

"Well . . ." Christine looked around for somewhere to sit, her knees suddenly weak under his insistent interrogation.

"I think I know that answer already, but I want to hear your justification. I'm sure you have one."

Christine fell in a heap on one of the couches. "Andrew asked me to come."

"You're still doing whatever he asks of you. I thought you assured me you were free of the Hanover domination."

"He was very confused about your abrupt departure. He wanted to know the status of the project and he wasn't free to travel right now, and since I was coming to the mainland on business anyway, he asked me to come in his place. You haven't answered any of his letters, so we felt Mr. Hicks was the one who could tell us what was going on."

"And did he?"

"Yes, he says you've canceled the book, and I'm so glad, Nick. I want to thank you . . ."

She started to stand up and go to him, but an imperious hand held up in front of him stopped her in her seat.

"I've quit the project for my own reasons, not in response to any of your clever entreaties."

"All I've ever asked is that you be fair, and consider the effect of the book upon the family involved."

"And do you think you've played fairly?"

"I've tried to," she said, feeling almost faint beneath the

force of his antagonism. Couldn't he see how he was hurting her? The book was no longer an issue; couldn't they begin their relationship again, without that conflict between them?

"I don't think it was fair for you to sneak behind my back to see my publisher. Any more than it was fair to try to deflect me by pushing that book idea about your alcoholism project. Don't you think I could see the potential of that idea for myself?" He suddenly lowered his voice. "And was it fair to invite me to your apartment to tempt me with that beautiful body of yours?"

Christine wanted to defend herself, make him see things from her standpoint, but she felt completely defeated, powerless in the face of his contempt. She could fight back at insults from anyone else, but from him they were too wounding to combat. She felt a rush of indignation that turned her cheeks scarlet and made her breath come in ragged gasps.

It seemed so right to be here with him in New York, to be in his apartment, to be sitting on his couch. But the words he was saying were all wrong. He was seeing things completely unreasonably, and there seemed to her no way to change him. She pushed herself up out of the deep couch.

"I must go. I have a plane to catch," she said, determined to save her dignity by making him think she couldn't have stayed for lunch even if he had been as polite as his servant and invited her.

To her surprise the bright shine in his angry eyes suddenly dimmed, and his stiff shoulders relaxed as he stepped across the room closer to her. His voice was almost as gentle as an island breeze when he spoke again, looking intently at her upturned face.

"The idea was doomed from the start. Your David Hanover, for all his interesting idiosyncrasies, just wasn't enough of a man to fill an entire book."

"I'm sorry you wasted so much of your time," she said, but he wasn't listening.

"What I still want to know, Christine, is this. Was David Hanover enough of a man to fill your life? My readers wouldn't give a damn, but he still fascinates me. I want to know if he ever properly loved you. You were an innocent schoolgirl when you met him. Did he teach you the sweet torments of wanting and giving and getting love? Were you loved, Christine?"

His voice was powerful in its musky softness. The gentler his voice, the more enraptured she became, not listening to the sense of his questions, only responding to the old seduction of his compassion.

She was tempted to tell him the truth. She wanted to say to him, "No man has ever truly loved me. You are the only one who could do that, for I would love you with all my heart in return." She wanted to curl herself against his broad chest, cling to him, and appeal to his sympathetic nature, pleading for his love. But she was too proud, had too strong an image of herself now to consider such helpless supplication. All she could think of was delaying her departure so that she might steal an extra moment or two under the soft glow of his forgiveness.

"All your questions about David Hanover are irrelevant now, aren't they? I mean, Mr. Hicks tells me you've begun another book already."

"Yes, I leave next week for Tokyo to begin my research there."

They were standing so close together that her breasts, safely protected by the stiff facade of her yellow jacket, touched lightly against his chest. Their eyes were locked together as their breathing began to come in unison, so intent were they upon each other. But neither reached forward to translate into physical gestures that need for the other. No hand was raised, no lips moved in search, no advantage was taken of this last opportunity to trade the raptures they could offer one another. The very air around them seemed electrified with the suppressed passion of the moment.

Christine felt a shudder begin deep inside her, heating the skin of her thighs and groin, and then invisibly shaking her thumping heart around inside her body so that she was afraid her restrained partner could see the torture she was feeling. How she longed for his touch, for those lessons in love that he sensed had never been given to her, that she wanted only from him.

Just when she was about to break the barrier of misunderstanding and reach out to him, there was the harsh interruption of a doorbell, and he sprang away from her as if he had awakened to find himself at the edge of a precipice.

"Come in, Iris," he said as he opened the door. "You're right on time."

Christine turned to see a sturdy matron in her early fifties stride into the room, one arm stacked high with papers and notebooks and folders, and the other supporting a half dozen thick library books, marked with protruding pieces of torn-up white paper.

"I see you have company," the woman said as she marched past them with her load. "I'll just take all this into the office and get it sorted out." And with a businesslike lack of interest in Nick's visitor, the researcher disappeared into the other room.

Christine tried to take consolation in the fact that the romantic luncheon set up in Nick's apartment had taken on a new and less threatening aura now that she'd seen his efficient co-worker in person. But she couldn't cope with the hopeless desolation she was feeling at the thought of leaving this apartment, walking away from Nick's New York home.

"I guess I should go," she said, "and let you get to your lunch meeting."

She tried to think of an excuse to stay, and she thought for one wild moment of fainting, or tripping on the way to the door and twisting her ankle. But she wasn't up to such an acting performance, and she walked toward the door slowly, without feigning any problems.

"You say you're going to Japan next week?" she asked, thinking of it as a tragedy that he would be passing that close to her life. "Does that mean you'll have a stopover in Honolulu?"

"Yes, just an overnight until I catch the next flight out to Tokyo."

Christine stalled for time, hoping some inspiration would come to her. "Will we see you?" she asked with the careless sound of a casual friend.

"What do you mean?" he asked.

Her mind raced in circles, searching for an idea. "I mean that I'm sure Mrs. Hanover and Andrew would like to meet with you. Uh, they would like to show you they harbor no hard feelings over the results of the project. How about coming out to the house and having dinner?"

Her heart almost stopped its incessant drumming as she waited for his reaction to her audacious invitation. Love had certainly made her bold! She wasn't at all sure that the Hanovers had any desire ever to see him again, but if he agreed, she was sure she could then convince them that it was the right thing to do.

Nick looked thoughtful. "You know, that might just be a good idea. There are a few things I'd like to say to those in-laws of yours. And now that we're not working together I could speak quite frankly. Would Jenny be there too?"

Christine's face froze for just an instant. "I'm sure I could arrange that. When she hears you're back on the island, I'm sure she'll make herself available at once."

"Good! You've got a date. Meet me at the airport on the evening of the eighteenth and I'll be glad to come for dinner."

Christine could barely contain the flip-flop feelings that were going on inside her chest. Her heart was dancing with excitement over the fact that she would see Nick again. Without that assurance, she doubted whether she could have left New York, or paid any attention to the meetings ahead of her with the NASAP leaders in Florida. But now she had something to live for, a hope to cherish, an open doorway through which she could send all her flights of fantasy winging. Now the calendar for the rest of her life went only as far as the eighteenth of the month.

"*Aloha*, Nick. See you in Hawaii," she whispered, her throat thick with emotion, just before she left his apartment.

CHAPTER TEN

THOSE WHO KNOW Honolulu well go shopping for their flower leis in Chinatown. On the day Nick was due to arrive at the airport, Christine left her office a little early and headed for Maunakea Street and Cindy's Lei Shoppe. She wanted this flower offering to be special, symbolic of all the sights and smells of Hawaii.

She strolled past the low buildings with their elaborate window and cornice trims and colorful sidewalk awnings, taking the time to appreciate this glimpse into another culture. People in old-country dress chattered in their native language as they walked by her, and tourists studied the displays in the open-air fish markets, the produce and herb stores, the noodle factories and the confectioners.

Christine looked over the exotic array of merchandise in the windows of the import stores and finally couldn't resist the temptation any longer. She went into a shop and bought a pair of earrings of dark green jade shaped like tiny leaves.

"No, I don't need a box for them. I'll wear them right now," she told the clerk, bending toward the counter mirror to put them on. She brushed her sun-lightened hair back from her face and fastened on the earrings. She noticed how flushed and eager her face looked in the mirror, her eyes almost feverish with intensity as the moment she had awaited finally was drawing near.

On the street again, she felt more confident wearing

something new. Nick might notice the touch of green at her earlobes, but even if he didn't, she would know that she was wearing something different, and that would give her the upbeat air she wanted to convey. It was important to her that he not see her looking unhappy. Though she had lost the most important thing in her life—his presence—she mustn't let him see her mourning that loss.

"I want one made completely of red ginger—that smells so good," she told the boy who was selling the long chains of fresh flowers. "And I have to have one of carnations and orchids, because he gave me one like that once."

"Your lover a pretty lucky guy," the boy said, carefully wrapping the leis she'd chosen in swirls of light tissue paper.

"And maybe just one more, of aloalo, the official flower of the Hawaiian Islands," she said.

"How about one to wear yourself?" he asked her with a smile. "A pretty *wahine* like you should have gardenias around your neck."

Christine remembered the huge gardenia for her hair that Nick had given her on their first date. It was still pungent, pressed between the pages of one of her favorite books, though by now quite brown with age.

"No gardenias, thank you. I think I have flowers enough right here," she said, laughing to the boy as she paid him.

But when she had to walk by the long row of flower stalls lining the entrance to the airport, she decided she didn't have enough flowers yet, and she bought Nick three more strands. He was a tall man, she reasoned, and it would take a lot of flowers to fill the space between his shoulders and ears; furthermore, the abundance would make him appear overwhelmed with welcome in the proper Hawaii tradition.

She heard the announcement over the public address system that his plane had landed, and she unwrapped the leis from the flower shop and draped them over one arm along with the new ones she'd just bought. She felt like the King Kamehameha statue at the Iolani Palace. Each year, on his day in June, the citizens draped his figure with so many flower garlands that his long outstretched bronze arms almost disappeared.

She strode rapidly back and forth to ease her nerves. As she made one quick turn on her heels and started to pace back across the waiting room she bumped right into a presence so large and compelling that she knew right away who it was.

"Hey, watch out who you're rushing into, little flower girl," Nick teased, grasping her upper arms to cushion their collision.

"*Aloha*, and welcome to Hawaii," she said, affecting the gentle and warm manner of a true Hawaiian by speaking softly and smiling broadly. And then, completely forgetting the flower-draping ceremony she had prepared for so elaborately, she threw herself against him, and let him take her into a strong embrace.

"Look out, you're getting all tangled up," he laughed as the strings of flowers caught between their arms and bodies.

Christine was embarrassed. "Oh, I almost forgot. This comes first and then the hug. Lean down now," she instructed.

"Are all those for me? Good heavens, Christine. I won't be able to see where I'm going. You'll have to lead me out of here."

And he was almost right: with the five thick rows of flowers around his neck, he was barely able to lift his chin above them. Christine stared up at him, relieved to see that his ocean-colored eyes were still available for her enraptured study, and his lips could just be seen twitching with amusement above the slender red blossoms of the ginger.

"Now comes the good part, as promised," Nick said then, and this time she didn't need to encourage his embrace. Heedless of the bruising he was giving the flowers, he took her into his arms, and they were crushed close amid the swirling scent of a variety of blooms. She looked up into his eyes with the longing of the remembered days and nights when she'd been without him. Then she reached both hands up tenderly to his face, pushed the flowers aside, and closed her eyes, reaching for his lips with her own.

They paid no attention to the traffic of people around them, the jostling they received as luggage and parcels bumped them, the jabber of conversation shouted past them,

the stares of sentimental older tourists on second honey-
moons trying to recapture just this kind of passion. They
kissed with all the pent-up fire they might have expressed
if they'd been alone on a deserted beach.

If only he was arriving to stay for good, her mind raced.
*If only he wasn't just passing through, on his way to an
assignment that will keep him too busy to think of me ever
again. If only he had come to stay here with me forever in
this paradise, where the sweet smells of carnations and
gardenias and ginger and pikake always fill the air.*

As his warm mouth explored deeper between her slowly
relaxing lips, she did not plunge into forgetfulness. Usually
when in his arms she let herself whirl away into a hallu-
cinatory world of pleasurable sensations. But this time she
kept herself alert to every feeling, memorizing it and storing
it up for the days ahead.

Nick drew back from her just enough to sever the kiss,
but kept his lips lightly brushing against hers as he spoke.
"I think we're in someone's way," he said.

"I don't care," she mumbled back to him.

"I think you've given me enough thank yous, for now,"
he said. With their lips still touching, each word he spoke
was like the start of a tantalizing new kiss, begun and then
withdrawn before she could grasp it.

"I'm not thanking you for anything," she said, mimicking
his way of speaking, almost babbling as she mouthed the
words tightly against his lips.

"Then what do you call this passionate ceremony?" he
asked, nibbling at the corner of her mouth as he finished
the question.

"We call this a typical airport welcome," she laughed
softly, and she could feel the movement of a smile beneath
her lips. Then she drew back from him for a breath, knowing
that her face was damp with a fine glow of perspiration as
if she had just emerged from a steamy greenhouse full of
flowering plants.

"Well, I've been greeted at a lot of airports in my day,
but I've never enjoyed a touchdown quite as much as this
one," he said, smiling down at her as he took her elbow

and turned her out of the crowd. "Is your car parked out this way?" he asked.

As she nodded in answer to him she began to consider what he'd said just a few minutes ago. Then she asked, "What did you mean, saying that I was thanking you?"

"Isn't that what brought on the outburst of emotion? I assume you're just as grateful as Andrew and his mother that I've dropped the project and this is your little way of saying so."

"You've made a mockery out of it," she said, lowering her head so that he wouldn't see the devastated expression on her face.

"Out of what?" he asked as they strode down the long corridor full of people.

"Out of a simple, native custom. That's all it was. I wanted to give you an island welcome. It's such a charming custom. It was done out of love, not gratitude for some favor done, or any other complicated motive." How much more clearly could she say it?

"Aren't you happy with my decision about the book? When I saw you in New York you seemed relieved to have found out from my publisher that the deal was off."

"I was relieved because I knew that my last mission for the Hanovers had been successfully accomplished. I knew that they would be happy, and that's why I seemed so relieved."

"Your last duty to the Hanovers, huh?" He gave her a skeptical, sideways glance. "And as for you, I suppose it didn't matter whether I went ahead with the book or not."

"I would prefer that the book not be written, but if you did write it, I know that it would be truthful, and I'm no longer afraid of the truth."

"Wow! Those are big brave words."

"And I hope you believe them."

Over the broad neckpiece of flowers his scrutinizing stare followed her as she surged ahead of him in the crowd to lead the way to the car.

*   *   *

At the Hanover house they were led right to the living room by a beaming Mrs. Wang.

"So nice to see you, Missy Hanover. You not been here for a very long time."

"I thought you were probably out here a lot," Nick said when the housekeeper had left the room. "You invited me to dinner here just as if this were your home again."

"What? Oh, not really."

Christine was walking slowly around the room, distracted by her remembrances of the years she'd spent confined in this unhappy house. "I'd forgotten that the drapes are always drawn in here." Her words were spoken in a monotone. "Just like the shutters in the dining room are always closed. It's so gloomy in here," she said, almost to herself.

"Then I guess you really haven't been here very much lately, if you've forgotten that," he said and she jumped at the sound of his voice, for any normal speaking tone seemed like shouting in these rooms. The atmosphere was like that of a tomb, where one respectfully whispered.

"How could I have lived in this stifling atmosphere?" she asked, not expecting an answer from him. For after all, Nick was the one who had shown her just how unbearable her life had been. He had shown her the color and excitement—and love—that life outside these walls consisted of.

Christine shuddered with revulsion as she glanced at the pictureless walls, the empty vases, the tables without books or magazines on them. It was more a temple than a home. It was consecrated ground, not for the comfort and enjoyment of the living, but devoted to the remembrance of the dead. And the long hallway outside, where Nick had deposited one of his flowered leis around each of the portraits of the family military men, was the sacred altar where her undeserving young husband had joined that legacy of heroes.

She tried to shake herself free of the austere mood of the place.

"Tell me about this trip of yours to Japan," she said, nervously perching on the edge of an upholstered chair.

Sensing her discomfort, Nick lapsed into his most dra-

matic style of commentary, describing for her all he planned
to see, the important people he planned to interview, the
information he needed to extract for his next book. She was
fascinated, as always, by his vivid descriptions of his work.
But despite all his concerned efforts to lift her spirits, she
was still distracted, quite overcome by those anxious feelings that prowled just below her level of consciousness,
produced by her presence in this stultifying environment.

With Nick gone forever from her life, would she ever
be tempted to return to the Hanover family circle, seeking
their companionship and a heritage of shared experiences?
Would her loneliness become so painful that she might
become willing to pay the price? Might she forfeit her freedom, become Mrs. Andrew Hanover, just so she wouldn't
be alone?

She stood up suddenly, stopping Nick in mid-sentence
with her sudden, erratic move.

"I'm sorry. Don't stop. Please go on, please!"

Nick resumed his narrative, but now Christine was listening to the sound of slow footsteps in the hallway outside.
Mrs. Hanover and Andrew were coming to join them in a
minute and she would no longer be alone with Nick. Mrs.
Hanover and Andrew were coming to take over her life, to
suffocate her in this cheerless graveyard. One hand flew to
her throat as she began breathing faster, a smothering feeling
of panic strangling her. Nick was going away. He was free
to fly off to see the world, explore the unknown, and she
was trapped forever, here in this elegant prison.

"Take me with you," she said.

"What did you say?"

Nick looked as if he couldn't believe he'd heard her
correctly. Christine had crossed the room to stand directly
in front of him, and she had reached out to grab his sleeve
with a desperate clutching motion.

"Take me with you. To Japan, anywhere. Just take me
with you away from here."

"Christine, you're shaking. Don't be afraid."

Nick heard the footsteps outside the door too, so his
embrace was quick and secretive, more like the reassuring

clasp of a friendly uncle at a family funeral. When the doors opened and Andrew led his mother and daughter into the room, Nick and Christine were standing separated by a perfectly decorous few feet of space. Only the most discerning eye would have caught the dazed look of surprise on his face, or the distress on hers, and none of the Hanover clan had been blessed with that degree of perceptiveness.

Andrew, after greeting Nick warily, went to fix everyone the customary drinks. Mrs. Hanover, after thanking Nick for coming, took her regular chair. And Jenny, after giving Nick the uninhibited kiss on the cheek that only a teenager can so shamelessly bestow, fluttered around close to his elbow, flattering him with dozens of questions throughout the cocktail hour.

Christine sat primly in her chair, and after Mrs. Hanover gave her that habitually critical look, she crossed her ankles and wrists at the exact point Mrs. Hanover had taught her and then sat watching Nick and Jenny like someone's maiden aunt. She remembered the energizing anguish of the jealousy she had felt that day when she had watched them on that boat tour. That was when she had first realized that she loved him, she thought, a misty expression softening her features. Nick obviously enjoyed Jenny's company; she could see that as she watched him. His manner with her was open and casual, with none of the sudden outbursts of anger that marked Christine's own moments with him.

Now with time to consider it, she regretted her foolish outburst of just a few moments before. What must Nick have thought of her, making such an audacious plea, dramatically begging him to sweep her away from all this, like Lois Lane calling out for Superman? Her hopeless attachment to him had made her act ridiculous, and she was mortified as she remembered the shocked look that had flashed across his face. Even now he was sneaking her an occasional glance, his dark eyebrows quizzically rising above his deep-set eyes, his whole expression indicating that he was still trying to figure out what had made her blurt out such a preposterous request.

What had made her think that she could, with mere determination, grasp at her own future and mold it to her own liking? She must force herself to be more resigned, to learn to settle for less than she'd hoped for her life.

Christine was glad when dinner was announced and she could get up and move. Mrs. Hanover had planned a sumptuous meal for her important New York guest, with filet of island mahi mahi poached in a light white wine sauce, crisp Maui onion rings, and a salad of Polynesian fruits flavored with kirsch. Everyone gave Mrs. Hanover repeated plaudits over the perfection of the meal, a perfection Christine knew was in celebration of Nick's cooperating with the Hanover's wishes.

Over coffee and cookies in the living room after dinner, the conversation livened up a bit. The Hanovers had finished with all their polite thank yous to Nick for looking into the project so earnestly, and had indicated convincingly their agreement to his decision that it might not make a very good book after all. Now Nick had absorbed all their very proper conversation, and he threw himself down in the Queen Anne chair that was normally reserved for the matriarch of the family, and cast a look around the room at everyone with a mischievous glint in his eyes.

"I may not see any of you again soon, if ever. So I have nothing to lose by speaking to you very honestly. If you hate me for this, so be it. But the reason I came here tonight was to get a few things off my chest."

The air in the room vibrated from the sudden tension. As Mrs. Hanover stood in the center of the room, unwilling to compromise by sitting anywhere else but in her favorite chair, her back suddenly stiffened at this hint of some sort of rude behavior about to contaminate the deathly tranquillity of her home. Her unyielding posture indicated that she disapproved of outspokenness in public, and would stop Nick's further comments if she could, but he immediately rushed on.

"If you'll pardon this frankness, Andrew, I hope that this failed book project has taught you a lesson."

Andrew looked up with surprise. Nick continued.

"It's time for you to get on with your own life now, don't

you think, and to stop trying to relive your brother's? You
need to find a new wife all your own, and interests and
pleasures of your own. Remember when you were young,
and you rejected the military career that was a family tradition, and developed your own identity as a successful
banker? That's the kind of independence you must find
again.''

Andrew looked outraged at such personal comments on
his life from a virtual stranger. But he must have known
inside that the words spoken were true, for rather than de-
fending himself with the useless rationalizations that Christine expected, he got busy with his cigarette package, making a great show of crumpling cellophane and thumping the
box on a table to extract a cigarette. Finally he mumbled,
"Good point," into a cloud of smoke he'd blown over his
head, and then sat studying the swirls with grave attention.

"And Jenny," Nick said, startling everyone with his swift
change of direction. "Come here."

He reached one hand out to her and she came rushing
to sit down on the floor beside his feet. Christine leaned
forward to listen intently, as curious as the smiling girl to
know what personal message required her close presence.
Nick continued.

"While I've given your father a hard time for being so
one-directional, for forgetting about his own life, you have
quite a different problem. You have given yourself no direction whatsoever, and all you ever think about is your
own life. I think you've spent quite enough time sunning
yourself and going to parties and bragging that first your
mother and now your father have no control over you.
You've wasted too much time lounging around having fun
and supposedly trying to decide what to do with your future.
Now it's time to make the step and go to college. It's the
best place to find that magical something you can build your
life around. That's how your father found his way into the
banking world."

"But Nick, you said you loved being with someone so
fun-loving. You said you envied me my carefree life." The
girl revealed herself as the young whiner she really was,

stubbornly trying to draw from the man the compliments she had become used to. But Nick would not play her game.

"Party time is over, Jenny. A little self-discipline wouldn't hurt you one bit."

There was a pause, and then he turned to look at Christine, who was sitting nearby in a state of suspended animation, astounded at hearing the raw naked truth spoken in this house, where legend and fantasy and fables were everything.

"Of course, when I suggest some self-discipline for Jenny, I don't mean that she should overdo it like Christine," Nick continued. He was clearly enjoying this chance to set the score straight. "When I first saw this vibrant, cheerful young woman she was holding herself under such tight control that it was obvious she was trying to play a part, pretend to be someone she was not. The Hanover family had pushed her into such an unreal world that when I came along and showed her a way out of it she was desperate to escape. She had to physically move out of this house, change herself with new clothes and a new hairstyle, cut herself off from this family, in order to be herself again. And that's a great pity. In her desperation to leave one world, she could very easily have thrown herself into a new and equally dangerous one."

Christine stared at him. So that was how he interpreted her whispered, "Take me with you"—the frantic scramblings of an escapee, looking about for any life raft. But then he didn't know she was in love with him.

She waited for the further attacks from him. So far, she'd come off easier than the others in the room, but she was certain he wasn't through with her. Then, like an arrow changing direction in mid-flight, his attention shifted.

"You are to blame for all this, Mrs. Hanover."

Christine's head whipped up to give the woman a worried look. No one spoke frankly to Mrs. Florence Hanover. The woman's whole life was built on dreams of past glory. If Nick were to rip them out from under her, the castle might collapse. What was he going to accuse her of? What would he tell her? Surely he wouldn't let this combative mood lead him to tell her the truth about David? He couldn't be that cruel.

"I know what you want to say to me, Nicolas," Mrs. Hanover said, brushing away the glimmer of a tear that must have formed as she'd been listening to his comments to the others. Everyone in the room was suddenly still, watching the lady battle to restore her profound sense of self-dignity as she stood alone in the center of the room.

"You are a young man who sees the truth, and isn't afraid to speak it, no matter what the consequences."

"Mrs. Hanover," Christine began, and got up to go to the woman, but a gesture as crisp as a military salute rejected her solicitude, and Christine went back to her chair.

"I'm sorry for what Christine turned into while she lived here with me. Now that I see her so changed, I realize that I was making her old before her time. But believe me, Christine, it was done with the best intentions. I wanted you to have the backing of a proud family tradition behind you, something I never had myself when I was young. I was ashamed of my family until I married Admiral Hanover and made his family background my own."

Christine stared at the woman, aghast. "You never told me that."

But the woman did not want to pursue her own sad story, which she obviously preferred to have remain untold. "I didn't want you ever to know the full truth about David. I didn't want you to become ashamed of carrying the Hanover name."

Christine's eyes widened with surprise. The woman knew a great deal more than she let on about her weaker son, it seemed.

Christine said, "I accepted the truth about David soon after I married him. But after he died, I blocked all that out, because I didn't think you knew. I thought you could only accept an idealized picture of your son."

"Oh, I knew, my dear. I knew only too well. He was very much like my own father, you see, so I recognized the pattern from the very first. But I was too proud to acknowledge it openly to anyone else, and usually not even to myself. I was hoping we could find some eager-to-please writer who would help us hide the truth forever with a book of praise about David. But instead we bumped up against this stubborn Yankee." She gave a bitter smile in Nick's direction.

"Knowing the truth about David, and accepting it within the family, doesn't mean you have to sacrifice your own pride, Florence," Nick said, and Christine marveled that he could speak to her so familiarly when she herself still could not bring herself to use her mother-in-law's first name. "As I told Christine on the day we visited the cemetery, you can walk tall, and be proud. You did the very best you could and you can take pride in that. Whatever David was, or whatever he did, was his own problem, and it is gone with him. You can only be judged on how you live your own life. And a life devoted to false idolatry, to maintaining a facade, is wasted."

Jenny was the first to break the heavy spell of shared emotion that filled the room.

"Well, I've had enough of all this soul-bearing and sobbing about. I'm going to make my weekly phone call to my mother." She flounced out of the room with obvious distaste for the self-examination that had been required of all of them in the last few moments.

"Well, you've accomplished something with all your brutal honesty, Nicolas." Andrew gave a short laugh. "That will be the very first time this summer that she's made her promised 'weekly' phone call to her mother!"

There was an awkward silence in the room, and a feeling that everything that could be said had already spilled forth.

"I think I've overstayed my welcome, with all this serious stuff," Nick said then, rising to his feet.

"I'll run you back to your hotel. You fly out to Japan in the morning, don't you?" Andrew asked, reaching into his pocket for his car keys.

"Christine, you drive Nicolas," Mrs. Hanover said, giving her daughter-in-law her usual commanding look, softened by just the hint of a wink. "My son and I have a lot to talk about. I hope we are strong enough people to make sensible use of all this food for thought that was served up tonight."

"Along with a wonderful dinner, I might add. I want to thank you again for that, Florence. You are a gracious hostess and you've taken my presumptuous comments with the bearing of the true lady that you are," Nick said with an ingratiating smile and handshake Christine found a bit exaggerated. Apparently he believed in serving up a touch of honey with his sour medicine.

Christine flustered about, looking for purse and keys and sweater, delighted that she would have another few moments alone with Nick but confused by all the rapidly changing currents that had flowed through the room. She didn't know quite what she wanted to say to him, except to apologize for her rash statement before dinner.

"You come over again, soon, Christine," Mrs. Hanover said as she walked the couple to the front door. "Not for any official functions or anything. Just because you are family and we want to see you."

"Thank you, Mrs. Hanover," Christine said, suddenly aware with deep gratitude that she probably wouldn't be afraid in the future to come here for a visit now and then. After all, she shared a great deal with this woman, who kept secrets so well. They had both learned to walk tall in spite of how David had betrayed them.

But as she gripped the woman's thin shoulder in farewell, she realized that she still wasn't ready to go so far as to call her mother-in-law "Florence," as Nick did so easily.

Nick drove, so that it was some time before Christine became aware of how much traffic there was on the road around Diamond Head and into Waikiki. She was too busy thinking about all that Nick had said, and how he had accused her of grasping at him as a means to freedom. Should she try to set him straight before he left here for good? Would he believe her if she told him that she loved him, that all she dreamed of night and day was being with him, going wherever he might go, sharing his life in New York, Tokyo, or Honolulu. Her statement had come not from a reckless woman, but from a woman in love. And a woman who had at last learned to take her destiny into her own hands.

"Where did all this traffic come from at this time of night?" Nick was muttering. "It looks like everyone on the entire island has come out for a drive at Waikiki tonight. If they're not careful, the island may tip right over." Christine could see his smile through the flicker of headlights flashing through the car. Then his mood turned more serious.

"That's the fourth police car that's passed me," he said. "I wonder what's going on. There must be a terrible accident up ahead."

"Or some sort of emergency," she speculated. "Look up on those roads into the hills."

Nick looked where she was pointing. Long rows of cars were heading up and away from the city, their tail lights leaving a bright and orderly trail of tiny red blinking dots behind them, like a string of Christmas lights.

On their right now was a residential district, and Christine could see several police cars cruising through the streets there, the revolving lights on their roofs casting strange shadows. She opened her window and could hear the loud and blurry sound of voices over bullhorns, but she was too far away to be sure of what she was hearing.

"They're saying something about 'evacuate,' I think," she said, her voice a bit shaky with fright.

"Turn on the car radio, will you, and see if you can get some news?" Nick said.

As she fiddled with the dials he began thinking out loud. "I heard someone on the plane discussing an earthquake today in Alaska. I didn't think much about it at the time, but you know . . ."

"Tsunami!" she said, completing his thought. She, too, had heard rumors during the afternoon. Whenever there was an earthquake in the Pacific region, which was frequent, Hawaiians worried about the repercussions of a tidal wave striking their shores some hours later.

The static crackle and long pauses gave her the clue at once that the radio stations had been replaced by an Emergency Broadcast System. Instructions were being given for everyone near the coasts to move to higher ground. The announcer informed the listeners that there was no need for alarm, as it was hoped there would only be a rise of six to twelve inches in the tide, but Christine remembered times past when some coastal cities had taken a real beating from waves traveling from thousands of miles away across the sea toward their shores at speeds of hundreds of miles an hour.

They pulled up in front of Nick's hotel, right behind a bus being loaded with unconcerned tourists. The locals were well trained in how to calmly and quickly move everyone to higher ground whenever there was any threat, and most of the travelers took it as something of a lark, sampling some more of the excitement of island living.

Nick leaned out to question one of the hotel staff he knew. "When is this thing scheduled to hit us, if it comes?"

"They say in about an hour, so you have plenty of time. Take a nice drive up Pali Highway and look at the stars. Nice night for it."

Now Christine could hear the blast of the city sirens that sounded intermittently to warn everyone. She wondered about the Hanovers, then remembered that historical records and scientific studies had shown the Diamond Head area to be in less danger of flooding than the crowded hotel portion of the town. Mrs. Wang kept a radio on in the kitchen and by now had probably warned the family to take a little drive *mauka*, toward the mountains.

Christine's apartment, far inland above Pearl Harbor and in a high-rise as well, was probably quite safe. "I hesitate to suggest this, but shall we go to my place for a cup of coffee and wait out the disaster?" she asked him when he had finished questioning the hotel boy as intently as if he were covering this event for a newspaper.

"The National Guard will have so many roads blocked off it could take us all night to find our way there. Let's just do as the man suggested and head up the Pali."

"Whatever you say; you're driving," Christine answered

as he followed the flashlight directions of police at every intersection and began working his way out of the city.

Pali Highway traversed the rugged Koolau Range that formed the very spine of the island, and led toward the northern coast. As they climbed upward through dense rain forest foliage they passed the highway markers for Queen Emma's Summer Palace, and the Upside Down Falls. Just before they reached the tunnel that would have taken them toward the towns of Kailua and Kaneohe, they saw the exit marked Nuuanu Pali Lookout; Nick turned off onto the old two-lane winding road. They followed the lights of a chain of cars through a luxuriant forest of eucalyptus, bamboo, and philodendron until they reached the lookout point.

The parking lot was crowded with cars trying to turn around to find parking places and people strolling about enjoying the warm evening just as if they had not come here to escape possible danger, but purely for some midnight sightseeing.

Nick found a parking place right near the concrete observation platform and as soon as he had turned off the car engine asked, "Do you want to get out and look at the view?"

Christine needed to get out and stretch her legs to relieve her nerves. She was glad for an excuse to spend a few more minutes evading conversation, for she still hadn't decided just how much she should confess to Nick about her feelings. She wasn't sure he'd care to know there would be a girl forever pining for him here on this island.

"Hold on to that railing. The tradewinds come rushing through this gap in the mountain range and you can get blown around," Nick warned.

"I don't mind," Christine said, tossing her short hair about in the breeze.

"Say, have I told you that I like your hair that way?"

"You mean wind blown?"

"No, I mean shorter, and free of all the clips and pins."

It was too dark to see the details of the panoramic view of windward Oahu spread out below her, but the darkness made more menacing the story Christine had heard of the historic event that had taken place right here on this spot.

"Did you know," she asked with a shudder, "that this is where Kamehameha the Great drove his enemies over the cliff? They say that thousands of the defeated were either pushed or jumped to their death down to those rocks."

Nick whistled. "It must be a thousand feet down there."

"It was all part of his conquest of Oahu, and his campaign to unite the Hawaiian islands into one kingdom."

"What a grisly story. I bring you up to this romantic spot to look at the lights and the stars and you tell me war stories."

"You brought me up here so we would both escape the great tidal wave," she laughed as she corrected him.

Nick leaned down to put one forceful hand behind her back and push her toward the car.

"Come on, let's get inside, out of the wind. I want to talk to you, and this exciting event has given me the opportunity and the setting. I really did not want to just get out of your car at my hotel and then fly off to Tokyo tomorrow, out of your life forever."

"Why not?" she asked shyly.

"Because I've found out that you love me," he said, startling her as she stepped into the car.

When he had gotten in beside her she found the courage to ask, "And how did you find that out?"

"It was the way you greeted me at the airport, I guess. There was just too much gusto in it to be phony. And you had no more reason to pretend to be nice to me, anyway, since you already knew the book project was finished."

"Then all along you've thought that I only endured your presence because I was trying to win something from you, the cancellation of the David Hanover biography. I hope by now you know differently."

"Yes, I think my realization was confirmed rather nicely when you made that scandalous proposition to become my traveling companion, right before dinner tonight. Really, Christine. You shouldn't go around throwing yourself at men."

"I don't go around throwing myself at men. I was trying in my own silly way to let you know how I feel about you."

"And now I know."

"Yes, I'm afraid so," she said, her despondency beginning to grow. "There's not much to be done about it, I'm afraid."

"Oh, you're quite mistaken. I'm going to take you with me, as you so daringly proposed," he announced.

For a moment Christine felt a furious flutter of hope and excitement within her, and then she reminded herself he'd said nothing of love or marriage. No real commitment had been expressed. He was a wordly man, one who probably saw her impetuous proposal as the chance for an amusing lark. He was not a domesticated homebody, looking for love and marriage. He had raised her hopes for one wonderful moment, only to dash them on the rocks of disillusionment.

"Of course it was all a joke. I can't go with you," she said sadly, her dejection complete.

Nick reached over and picked up her nervously fidgeting hands, and wrapped one of his over them to still their movement.

"My darling. You are going to be with me from now on and forever more. How could you have missed the clues? How could you not have known how much I love you?"

"You love me?" she said haltingly, trying on the beautiful words for size.

"I love you and I want to marry you and I want to buy a beautiful house for you up on Mount Tantalus with a view of all Honolulu and I want . . . ."

"Oh, Nicolas Carruthers. I can't stand it. It is really too much to have all my dreams burst into bloom this way. Those are all the fantasies I've kept myself alive with these past few months. Are they really going to come true?"

He leaned awkwardly across the gear box and tried to embrace her.

"If we weren't in this two-person chastity belt, I'd show you in a minute what kind of dreams are going to come true for you. I'm going to love you as you've never been properly loved, my sweet. That's all I've ever wanted from the first day I saw you. It's been an obsession with me from the moment I heard that delicious laugh of yours bubble out of the austere little woman in black who appeared at my door. All I wanted to do was cut you loose from the grief, show you what you were missing out of life, set you free so that in time you could come to me and accept all the love that I have to give you."

"You did set me free. You taught me to love luaus, and poi dogs, and orchid leis, and silk dresses, and suntanning beaches. I'd forgotten what it felt like to love life and love myself. Then it was just a natural progression to fall in love with you."

From all around them car horns began honking and engines started up. Nick rolled down his window and looked out. A man hurrying to get into his car yelled at him.

"It just came over the radio. We can all go back; it's all clear. The tide only came up six inches."

"The crisis is over, everything is okay," Nick told her.

"You'd better believe it," she proclaimed with a clear tone of confidence in the future.

Just as Christine was fastening her seat belt, expecting Nick to start the engine so they could follow all the other cars down the mountain, she heard him open the door with an explosive energy, and step out into the confusion of departing cars around them. She leaned over to see what he was doing. Obviously, the confines of the small car were crowding his expansive mood, for he was standing swinging his arms back and forth as he looked up at the bright shower of stars above him. When she got out and went around to join him, he put his arms out to pull her against him. His eager plans for the future tumbled out impatiently.

"We don't have time for a big fancy wedding, you know. We're both too busy to take a lot of time out for those sentimental moments. If we get married right away you can come with me to Japan. That will be our honeymoon, if Kim will give you a week or two off."

"If it's for a honeymoon, she'll let me off."

Her head nestled against his shoulder, Christine pondered what their life together would be like. There would be Nick coming and going on assignments, there would be her own work, which was important to her, and the new house he'd promised her, where they would both come to be alone together in between. It would be an exciting life, almost everything she'd ever wanted, but she wondered whether the indomitable spirit of Nicolas Carruthers would ever allow itself to be tied down more firmly than that. It would be like two single people living together. He would consider it useless sentiment to plan on becoming a family in the true sense, where home became more than just a wonderful place they shared to live in. But she had no desire to further consider limitations to that ideal picture of their life together.

"Do those plans satisy you?" he asked her, bending his head downwards toward her, speaking as if all that mattered in the world was her happiness.

"I've never been so happy in my life," she said, and noticing that they were now almost alone in the rapidly emptying parking lot, she leaned forward expectantly for one of those kisses she could not get enough of.

In the mottled moonlight Nick's rippling dark hair seemed like rolling waves on a midnight sea, and Christine ran her fingers through it, stroking backward from his temples where she could feel the veins throbbing beneath her touch.

"The next time there's a tsunami warning, I promise I will be with you again just like this," he murmured. "You've brought out a nurturing and protective side to me that I never knew I had. I don't think I'll be spending much time traveling any more. All I want is to be with you."

Christine thought about the one thing more that would make her vision of the future with him complete, but she dared not voice it. Then, almost as if in answer to her prayers, came Nick's characteristic reading of what was on her mind.

"There would be only one thing that could add to our

happiness. That would be if the next time we come up here to see the view we bring a new little baby Carruthers along with us."

"Is that what you want? Would that make you happy?"

"I think that would pretty much permanently tie me to home and hearth, my darling."

Her eyes sparkled with the ecstasy of one who is about to see all her dreams come to fulfillment.

Nick looked at her with a crooked smile. "You still don't quite believe all this, do you?"

"I can believe anything now that I know you really love me," she answered.

The dark parking lot was now completely deserted, and it was like being alone on top of the world with him, the warm tradewinds swirling about them as they shared their dreams of the limitless future ahead of them.

"Let's go," he said suddenly. "We have a lot to do."

She remained pressed against him, eager to begin whatever was ahead of them, but reluctant to let this golden moment slip away.

"One more kiss to seal the bargain?" she asked.

"Hmm. Couldn't possibly say no."

What they had intended as a quick kiss captured them both completely. Christine clung to his lips with all the fervency of one unafraid to declare herself a captive.

At last Nick pulled away, wiping one hand across his forehead in a useless attempt to cool the excitement she'd aroused in him.

"You really are an unquenchable little wench, do you know that?" he laughed, grabbing her hand to lead her to her side of the car.

Then she whispered something so softly that he probably didn't hear it over the sound of the door slamming. "Only with you," she assured him. "You are the only one."

Introducing a unique new concept in romance novels!
Every woman deserves a…

You'll revel in the settings, you'll delight in the heroines, you may even fall in love with the magnetic men you meet in the pages of…

Look for three new
novels of lovers lost and found coming every
month from Jove! Available now:

___ 05907-2 ALOHA YESTERDAY (#10) $1.75
        by Meredith Kingston

___ 05638-3 MOONFIRE MELODY (#11) $1.75
        by Lily Bradford

___ 06132-8 MEETING WITH THE PAST (#12) $1.75
        by Caroline Halter

Available at your local bookstore or return this form to:

JOVE PUBLICATIONS, INC.
Dept BW, 200 Madison Avenue, New York, NY 10016

Please enclose 50¢ for postage and handling for one book, 25¢
each add'l book ($1.25 max.). No cash, CODs or stamps. Total
amount enclosed: $_____ in check or money order.

NAME_____

ADDRESS_____

CITY_____STATE/ZIP_____

Allow three weeks for delivery.   SK-20